AUSTIN

The K9 Files

Dale Mayer

AUSTIN: THE K9 FILES, BOOK 29
Beverly Dale Mayer
Valley Publishing Ltd.

ISBN-13: 978-1-778866-87-6
Print Edition

Books in This Series:

Ethan, Book 1

Pierce, Book 2

Zane, Book 3

Blaze, Book 4

Lucas, Book 5

Parker, Book 6

Carter, Book 7

Weston, Book 8

Greyson, Book 9

Rowan, Book 10

Caleb, Book 11

Kurt, Book 12

Tucker, Book 13

Harley, Book 14

Kyron, Book 15

Jenner, Book 16

Rhys, Book 17

Landon, Book 18

Harper, Book 19

Kascius, Book 20

Declan, Book 21

Bauer, Book 22

Delta, Book 23

Conall, Book 24

Baron, Book 25

Walton, Book 26

Cage, Book 27

Trey, Book 28

Austin, Book 29

Mateo, Book 30

Boxed Sets and Bundles

https://geni.us/Bundlepage

About This Book

Welcome to the all new K9 Files series reconnecting readers with the unforgettable men from SEALs of Steel in a new series of action packed, page turning romantic suspense that fans have come to expect from USA TODAY Bestselling author Dale Mayer. Pssst… you'll meet other favorite characters from SEALs of Honor and Heroes for Hire too!

Austin hates to think that Kat had tapped into his inner psyche and had pulled out the one job he both wants yet is terrified to do. He'd walked away—or maybe had been chased away from Rox. He is no longer sure; he only knows that he needs closure on a marriage that had been heaven, until it turned to hell. And now the same family he'd married into had gotten, then lost, a War Dog. And, sure enough, Kat had found out about his entanglement, asking him point-blank if it was time to get his life together.

Rox had sent Austin away in the red heat of temper, and he'd gone, as in gone and never to return. Now here he is, sitting in her kitchen as if they'd never had such a tumultuous past. Finding out he'd returned for the missing War Dog and not for her bit hard. Still, she'd called in about Cowboy, the missing dog, but hadn't expected them to send Austin. It's as if the gods weren't done ruining her life.

Finding the missing War Dog and sorting out the other unsettling issues on the ranch Austin had fallen in love with years ago isn't going to be easy—particularly with Rox at his side—but he knows he is fighting for more than just peace and justice. He is fighting for his—their—future. One that, deep down, he never truly let go of.

Sign up to be notified of all Dale's releases here!
https://geni.us/DaleNews

BADGER STARED AT his wife. "What the hell, Kat? I'm definitely not letting you work with anybody I want to keep local."

She smiled at him. "You already bitch and complain because you want to find more work for these men. You don't want any of them to suffer without enough to keep them going—even if it's not money that they actually need."

"Everybody needs self-esteem. Everybody needs to know that they're useful and that they still have something to offer this world," he declared.

Gently she touched the corner of his mouth and nodded. "I know, and that's only one of the many reasons I love you."

"Only one of the reasons?" he repeated, waggling his eyebrows. "Tell me more."

She burst out laughing and said, "No, I think your ego is doing just fine."

"You're the one who's doing just fine," he replied. "It's freaking unbelievable how on target you always are. It is uncanny."

"I don't know about that," she said. "Yet I'm so happy for Trey and Missy—and Silas and Schooner. And I'm happy that this crazy situation has a happy ending."

"What about Keith, the woman's son? Do you think

he'll get over it?"

"I don't know," Kat admitted. "It depends on how the community handles it. Keith may just sell his home and move away, but, then again, maybe he'll learn to fish," she teased, with a knowing smile.

Badger sighed. "Are we done now?"

At that, she laughed. "Do you really think we're done?"

"No, not likely," he muttered, "but you could consider it."

"No, we have two more files here, and then, chances are, we're done. At least that's all we have for now. I guess we'll cross that bridge when we get there."

"Two more files," Badger muttered, shaking his head. "I can't even imagine. Are you thinking you'll go for the goal?"

"Of course I'll go for the goal," she declared. "Two more. That's not much of a challenge, is it?"

"Sure it is. Where is this one?"

"Cowboy country."

"What do you mean, cowboy country?"

"The War Dog was going with a group who does pack trips, trail riding, and the like."

"And?"

"The War Dog went missing during the night."

He frowned at her. "And we're supposed to track him down? Will you also track down the bear that took him down too?"

She smiled up at him. "We do know one cowboy. He's a bit of a renegade, but I thought maybe somebody who used to do both horseback riding and training dogs might be okay to go to Texas. Plus, he's from there."

"Oh, don't tell me," Badger grumbled. "Austin is bound for Austin?"

She burst out laughing. "That's exactly what I was thinking. At least he could fly into Austin, but he wants to drive."

"Long way to go. He's testing the limit of your newest prosthetic, isn't he?"

"Don't we all?" She grinned broadly. "The ranch is in the backwoods, way south of Austin, somewhere closer to the border—or maybe closer to the Gulf of Mexico. I'm not sure, but it's a big cattle ranch, out in the middle of nowhere. The wife of the owner has a side gig with a pack string and trail-riding tours. Her son and her daughter run it with her."

Badger just nodded, as he watched Kat go deep in thought. He finally asked her, "And?"

"There's no *and*," she said, batting her eyelids at him. "No *and*s at all."

"What's the dog's name?"

She laughed. "You won't believe it."

"Probably not. What's the name?"

"Cowboy. They call him Cowboy."

"Oh, for crying out loud," he muttered, with a moan.

She nodded and laughed. "But he's also a beloved member of the team."

"And the War Department contacted you?"

"The family contacted the War Department, thinking they were in trouble because they lost the War Dog," she explained. "So, in that way, this is already unusual because they fessed up. *Hey, we don't know what happened, but it could be something bad.* So we just don't know much, and now the War Department wants us to look into it."

"That is all just too far-fetched."

"It is far-fetched, so let's just say the War Department may not really think there's any point looking into it, but I don't feel the same way." When Badger frowned at her, Kat shrugged. "I think he deserves a chance."

"Cowboy or Austin?"

She smiled. "Let's just say, … Austin was named Austin for a reason."

He pinched the bridge of his nose. "So, don't keep me in suspense. Does Austin know this ranching family already or something?"

"Or something," she said.

"You'll have to talk to him and see if he's willing to go."

"Oh, I'm pretty sure he's willing to go."

"And why is that?" Badger asked.

"Because that daughter who runs the side company … is also his estranged wife. It's apparently a marriage that's not working, but they haven't gotten the divorce paperwork done yet."

"Meaning?"

"Meaning that something is still there and needs to be worked out," she stated.

"Have you talked to Austin? What if he doesn't want to go?"

She nodded. "He's already on his way."

CHAPTER 1

AUSTIN MCFARLAND HOPPED out of his truck and slammed the door, and, yes, with a little more force than necessary. He had been arguing with himself the entire drive over here, across both states, calling himself stupid—and a host of other names—wondering what crazy magic Kat had that made this seem to be a good idea just hours ago. She'd convinced him so easily. Too easily. Something to do with closure and moving on, finding out what was really there, and all the rest of that crap. It made a lot more sense when he was talking to her, but, the minute he left, he was confused as hell.

He hitched up his jeans and took a careful step forward. After any long drive, the prosthetic was often okay, and yet occasionally it seemed as if a dozen little devils danced on the inside of his joints, causing all kinds of hell. Enough to make him hesitate for a moment before taking that first step every time. At the moment though, it felt pretty decent.

Austin took a few more steps toward the front door of the main ranch house that he knew so well. Just as he got there, the door opened, and a petite older woman stepped out, the surprise on her face quickly turning to delight as she opened her arms and raced toward him.

"Oh my gosh," Amie cried out, almost in a squeal.

He grinned as the tiny woman threw herself into his

arms and gave him a big hug.

She pulled back almost instantly, giving him a grin, her gaze dancing. "I didn't think we would ever see you again, son."

"I'm here," he stated. "It's nice to know I'm welcome."

"Of course you're welcome," Amie declared, giving him another big hug. "Just wait until Jake knows you're here." When Austin winced at that, she shook her head. "No, you've got no reason to be upset."

"Really?" he asked. "We were family … briefly."

She frowned, bringing her eyebrows together. "What do you mean, *briefly?* Are you guys divorced?" There was just enough fear in her tone that he had to wonder.

He shook his head. "Not yet."

"Then you're still family," she stated, with a firm nod.

He laughed. "Pretty slim ground for it though."

"It doesn't matter to me," she muttered. "You're still family." And, with that, she nudged Austin forward. "Come on now. Come on inside."

He let himself be moved along, as Amie pushed and dragged him into the old familiar farmhouse. He'd spent an awful lot of his days here—and a lot of his nights too, to be honest. As he walked inside, he looked around self-consciously, and Amie smiled at him. "She's not here."

He rolled his eyes. "That's the problem with coming back here, where everybody knows you and knows what happened."

"We don't know what happened," she exclaimed. "And believe me that a lot of us would love to know, but Rox isn't talking."

"No, of course not," he muttered to himself.

"And it doesn't look as if you'll be talking either." She

frowned at him.

"Nope," he confirmed, with a smile.

Amie snorted. "If you guys would just talk to each other, … you could probably get it all sorted."

She was probably correct, but that didn't mean Austin was willing to go in that direction, at least not right now.

"Come on into the kitchen," she urged him. "I've got coffee on."

He chuckled. "You always have coffee on."

She nodded. "I drink it pretty steadily myself, and you know Jake." She rolled her eyes. "He's a heavy coffee drinker, if you still remember."

"I figured he would be out with the team, checking out the land, all on horseback."

"Rox is doing a lot of that now."

"Good," he noted. "That's what she always wanted to do."

"It is," Amie agreed, "and she also really loves her family."

He nodded. "Yeah, I know that too. I wasn't trying to take her away from you."

Amie sighed, then nodded. "I know that, but I don't think she saw it that way."

He laughed. "No, she sure didn't," he stated, but he didn't add anything to it. Just some things wouldn't go the way Austin wanted. So it was best to not even get involved in that conversation, at least if he were smart.

She poured him a cup of coffee, and he took it with gratitude. "You're looking well," she shared.

"Maybe, at least on the outside."

She frowned as she studied him. "Are you okay?" Her facial expression turned more serious.

He smiled and nodded. "I'm fine."

Her frown deepened. Giving him a searching look, she asked, "Why do I feel as if you're not telling me everything?"

"Because I'm not telling you everything," he admitted, refusing to get into it.

She sighed. "There you go again, … keeping secrets."

"Hardly secrets," he said. "I'm just not about to spill everything in my world, especially when I haven't seen you in so long."

She walked over and gave him a tiny slap on the shoulder. "Now whose fault is that? We were family long before you became family, and you really hurt Jake when you walked."

Austin just nodded. Knowing there wouldn't be a happy ending to any part of this conversation, he wasn't sure what he was supposed to do or to say about it.

Amie walked back to the fridge and rummaged through it, bringing the cream over.

He smiled when he saw it.

She asked him, "You still take cream, don't you?"

"Yes, I do," he confirmed, "but this is fine. No need to make a fuss."

"You look good," she noted, studying his features closely, "tired though."

"Long drive."

"Where did you come from?"

"New Mexico."

Her eyebrows shot up. "Well, … that's some distance. You could have flown."

"I could have, but I wanted to bring my vehicle."

"Have you been to see your mom?"

He glanced down at the coffee cup in his hand and

shook his head. He heard the sad, gentle sigh coming from this tiny woman whose heart was so big that everybody else's problems were just too hard for her to handle sometimes. "She has remarried and living overseas and my father… well, who knows where he is."

"They do love you. You know that, right? They're your parents."

He looked over at her, a cocky smile on his face. Then, shaking his head, he muttered, "So you keep telling me."

"*Uh-oh*, what have they done now?"

"Nothing. … They would have to know something about me in order to be doing anything."

"And you haven't talked to them either, have you?"

"Nope, I sure haven't," he declared, with a smile. "I won't either."

Amie frowned at that, but just then came stomping footsteps through the front door, and Jake's bellowing voice called out, "Who's the company? I don't recognize the truck out front." He walked into the kitchen a few seconds later, took one look, and an immediate frown filled his face as he glared at Austin. "What the hell are you doing here?" he snapped.

Immediately Amie raced to his side in excitement. "Isn't it wonderful to see him?" she cried out.

He looked at her, then down at Austin, shaking his head. "Wait until Rox finds out."

"It's about time," Amie stated firmly. She might be tiny, but she was definitely the main force in this household.

Jake groaned. "You know damn well she won't like any of this."

"Oh, I agree that she won't like it, but they both need to face it. It is about time to sort things out."

"It's definitely time," Jake grumbled, giving Austin a hard look, "but it doesn't look as if he came on his hands and knees."

She snorted. "As if you would either."

"I have no intention of being on my hands and knees," Austin stated coolly as he stood up, "and I'm not here for Rox at all." The two of them stared at him in surprise. He shrugged. "Apparently you guys lost a War Dog."

At that, Jake snorted. "What's that got to do with you?"

"I'm here on behalf of the War Department," he shared, knowing that would be like spitting fire in everybody's face.

"Holy Hannah," Jake spat, staring at Austin. "You didn't come here for Rox, but you came for a dog?" He looked at him with fire and fury in his expression. His tone on the other hand was as cool as an iceberg. "Boy, you need a talking to."

"No, I don't," Austin countered. "I didn't come here for her because she made it very clear how she feels about me, … about being with me. Her answer was pretty clear. She kicked me out, so nothing is left there."

Even Jake winced at that. The fire was gone from his expression, just sorrow and resignation left behind. "She regretted it immediately," he told Austin, "but you were already gone."

"Sure, I was. I was leaving on a mission, something she knew very well," he snapped. "She didn't give me much choice, and, while you may feel differently—and blame me all you want—but you know the truth as well as I do. Rox annihilated everything that was between us. So, believe me when I tell you that I'm not here for her."

ROX STOPPED ON the front steps and froze, as she heard Austin's voice—both her dreams and her nightmares were hitting so close to home that it brought tears to her eyes. She couldn't believe Austin was here. She heard her father bellowing about something, but she didn't really understand until she heard the mention of a War Dog. Of course. … Austin was here about the dog, not her. A damn good dog, but it still hurt like hell.

She stared down at her dirty fingers and her torn nails, filled with dirt from an honest day's work in the fields. Her boots muddy, her jeans dirty, her body wearing a very unflattering shirt, she shook her head. Of course he wasn't here for her, and that's when she heard his words about her kicking him out. It was a knife to her heart.

Yeah, she had kicked him out, but she hadn't expected him to leave. Not to *leave*, leave, as in to never come back, to never contact her again, to never speak to her, with no forgiveness ever for her careless words. She hadn't expected this blankness, this void, this emptiness that she couldn't ever comprehend as so utterly final.

She had been young. Well, if twenty could be considered young. Regardless she had been apparently way too young to comprehend the enormity of what she'd done in the heat of that moment. She knew what the fighting had been about. It was about his going back out on a mission, and his telling her that she'd married a navy man first and foremost and that she had no business telling him that he would now be forced to change careers because she didn't like that he was gone all the time.

Her father had warned her ahead of the marriage that she wouldn't change that part of Austin and how it was a major part of who he was, but she, in her heart of hearts, hadn't believed it. She thought for sure that she would be enough to keep him home. It had been a shock to realize that she wasn't enough and that she would never ever be enough. She had married him knowing he was in the navy, but she just hadn't really understood what it meant to him. Somehow his obligations to the navy hadn't been something she'd considered before she married him. Nor afterward either. Not until the fight that had ended *them.*

Now she still lived here and worked here on the ranch, but she missed him constantly, every minute of every day.

Yeah, she'd been young, and the fight had been intense, and, when Austin had walked, he'd walked for good. It had broken her heart, and she'd been forever wounded after that point. She'd refused to even date anybody because, in her mind, she was still married and was still connected by her wedding vows. She'd never contacted him for a divorce in the last five years, but she'd grown up a hell of a lot.

She didn't know if he'd suffered at all because the one thing he had said when she kicked him out was that, if he left, if she was kicking him out for good, that was it, and he wasn't coming back. The fact that he was here now, and for a dog rather than her was doubly insulting, yet also very true to form.

He'd broken her heart once, and, while she might have been at fault, she'd taken a long time to heal, a long time to get back on her feet, and she wasn't that same delicate, naïve girl anymore. She didn't dare let anybody else take away that sense of control that she had taken so long to learn, that sense of independence and ability to stand on her own.

Only now as she looked back did she realize just how young she had been. It amazed her because, at the time, no way she could have seen it, and yet now, looking back? … It was an eye-opener. She'd also been the one who had insisted on marriage, and it had been a good marriage for a very short while—until she got tired of everything, and that was on her, not him. He'd given her a choice, and she'd taken it, and that was on her too. But now here he was, and somehow she had to walk inside that farmhouse and talk to him, even though everything in her wanted to turn and run.

The irony was that she was also the one who had called the War Department about the dog, and who did they send? They sent the very same junkyard dog that she had lost her heart to so very long ago. With a smile plastered on her face and steel in her spine, she walked in, slamming the door shut, thinking this would be one hell of a day.

She walked into the kitchen, then stopped and eyed him carefully. Damn, he looked good. Tired and maybe a little bit rougher around the edges, but he was still the same man who made her heart melt. He'd always been the one for her, but somehow she just hadn't realized that she wasn't the one for him. He looked over at her, tilted his head, and then turned the conversation back to her father, not so much cutting her out but ignoring her.

She sucked in her breath, her gaze turning to her mother, who stared at her with a hopeful expression on her face. Her mom was desperately hoping that something could be worked out, that this would blow over, and that everyone would be back together again.

Rox bit her bottom lip, strode over to where the coffee was, and said, "I hear you're looking for a dog."

"Yep. Apparently you lost him," he said, his tone calm, not even an ounce of emotion shown.

That fact gave Rox her first bit of hope.

CHAPTER 2

ROX DESERVED A medal for staying calm, controlled, and collected. She was really proud of herself for managing to sit through this act of civility, gathered around the table, sharing awkward tidbits about their lives, eventually discussing the missing War Dog with Austin. She had shared how she continued to listen for his barks in the nighttime, rode the ranch during daylight every chance she got—especially where the War Dog had last been seen. Rox loved all the animals on the ranch and beyond, but she had her favorites. Cowboy was one of them. She sighed.

By the time Austin stood up and looked at his watch, he announced, "It's late. I'll head into town, grab my motel room, and, if you're okay with it, I'll be back out in the morning, and I'll check out Cowboy's last movements."

"Can it wait that long?" Rox asked.

He turned to her. "You tell me. How long has the dog been missing?"

"A couple weeks," she admitted. "I'm the one who called the War Department because I'm really worried about Cowboy. He's a damn good dog, and, if you remember one thing, you should remember that I'm all about animals."

"I do remember that," he conceded, "and, from what I know of Cowboy, he should have decent survival training, so if he's got an opportunity to fend for himself ..."

"The thought that he might not have the opportunity to fend for himself is killing me," Rox admitted, trying hard to keep her voice even, but knowing that she was failing.

He caught the break in her voice, looked over at her, and gave her a nod. "Let's start now then," he suggested, as he sat back down again. He frowned as he looked at his watch again, then told Amie, "I don't want to interfere with your dinnertime, but this is important."

She waved him off. "That you would even worry about that in my house," she replied, "makes me very sad. And don't you even think about staying in a motel or insulting me by not staying for dinner," she snapped, glaring at him.

He stared at her for a long moment.

Rox realized the position he was in because Amie had always loved him. It had broken her heart when they had split.

Finally Austin gave her a nod. "Fine, thank you very much for your hospitality."

His tone was so formal that Rox watched her mother's gaze crinkle with a mix of hurt and pain.

Amie took a deep breath and nodded. "You're welcome." With that, she turned and marched herself into the kitchen.

Rox looked over at her father, staring at Austin with a puzzled smile. "Not too many men get away with that from Amie," he noted. "You were always the only one."

"I never tried to hurt anybody," Austin stated, as he stared at Jake. "I was only doing as I was told." With that and not even a look in Rox's direction, he pulled out a notebook. "Now let's get the details. Which one of you has been dealing with the War Dog?"

When Jake nodded toward Rox, she knew she would be

up next.

Austin twisted so he could face her. His first direct look at her was like a shot right through her gut.

She took a deep breath and began, "I was working with Cowboy on a daily basis. He was with me when we were out trail riding with guests or just working the ranch. Either way we were usually with two other guys, our ranch hands, Carlos and Raul. We had six visitors at the time," she added. "They were all from Switzerland. On day three, we got up in the morning, and Cowboy was just gone."

She bit her bottom lip, remembering the pain and the horror of realizing she would have to go back over all this again for Austin. "I spent as much time as I could searching the ranch for Cowboy, and I also sent Raul off to look for him. We called for him. We set out dog food in random places, but the wildlife would eat it if Cowboy didn't. We notified the local veterinarian, in case someone found Cowboy and brought him in to be looked over. We did everything possible that we thought of, but there was just no sign of him."

"Tracks? Bear, cougar, anything?"

"No." She looked over at her father. "Nothing. There was nothing."

Jake nodded. "When she says nothing, she means nothing."

Austin just looked at her and nodded.

He surely remembered that the animals were an important part of her life, and she was only dealing with visitors because it brought in the money that they needed to keep everything else going.

Things had been much better in the last few years, and a part of her wanted to ditch the whole tourist ranch thing.

But it still brought in money, and, after COVID had taken a hit to their pocketbooks, she didn't want to cause too much uproar and change things right now. She wanted to keep at the trail riding, until they were sure that they were over the hump and didn't need that side income.

Yet she also knew that it made no sense that Cowboy disappeared in the night.

Austin stared down at his notes, and Rox could see the wheels turning in his head. He'd always been really good at that sort of thing. Analyzing info, sorting out things, looking at all the possibilities, then coming up with something that nobody else ever thought about. As she settled back, she realized she felt a sense of relief, a sense of calm, because, if she trusted anybody to find Cowboy, it was Austin.

And, damn, that pissed her off.

THE CONVERSATION CONTINUED through dinner, less stilted now, but Austin didn't get much more in the way of information. He stayed and ate dinner, knowing full well that another fight would be coming, so he decided that he would defuse it right off the bat. It would mean staying around Rox, but, since she was being civil and more or less staying to herself over the entire ordeal, it was the least he could do to ease the strain still evident at the table.

When he got up to take his dishes into the kitchen, Amie followed him. "Your room is ready."

He stiffened ever-so-slightly, then looked at her and nodded. "As long as it's not the same room."

She smiled up at him. "It's not the same room."

He nodded. "Then that's fine, and … thank you for

your generosity."

She sighed. "I don't even know what went so wrong," she muttered, "but it broke my heart when you left without a word." He just nodded and didn't say anything. "However, I do understand from Rox that she didn't give you a chance."

He just nodded again and waited, knowing that Amie hadn't followed him into the kitchen, and she would have her say no matter what. He'd always respected her because she'd been fair and open and understanding of everything.

"I just want you to know that I don't know what's going on. I don't know what happened, and obviously I was devastated over the whole thing," she shared, "but I'm not one to hold a grudge. If there's anything you two have to work out, this is a really good time to do it. There," she declared, with a sigh, as she dropped the tea towel onto the counter. "Now that I've said my piece, I'll leave it for now, and I won't say any more."

He snorted.

She stopped, turned, and looked at him, caught the big grin on his face, and her face lit up with sheer joy. "You have no idea how much I have missed you." She walked over, gave him a great big hug again, and squeezed him really close. "I'm so damn sorry for whatever the hell happened." And, with that, she headed back into the dining room, calling out, "Who wants dessert?"

Jake asked, "Why are you even asking, Mama?"

She laughed as she brought out a pie from the sideboard that Austin hadn't even seen, realizing that it must be new. He sat back down at his same seat at the dining room table and glanced over at Rox. "Seems I'll be staying here."

Rox nodded. "She wouldn't have it any other way."

"Maybe not, but it's not what I intended."

"Of course not," she noted, a hint of mockery in her tone.

He studied her for a long moment and then just didn't say any more.

Finally she nodded and admitted, "You're handling this better than I am."

He shrugged. "I didn't know what to expect, and the least we can do is be civil."

"*Sure*," she replied, with that edge of mockery again.

He contemplated what to say and then decided that the prudent response here was to stay quiet. He ate his pie and focused his thoughts on Cowboy because that was the one thing he could do.

"How the hell did you get assigned to do this, anyway?" Jake asked, staring at Austin, still puzzled.

Austin smiled. "I'm good friends with Kat, who has been doing a lot of the organizing and search and rescue of missing War Dogs for the War Department," he replied smoothly. "She knew that I was from this area and thought I would be a good fit for finding Cowboy. She also knew about my naval history and has been creating my prosthetic," he shared, with a smile.

"History, prosthetic, what are you talking about?" Amie bounded to her feet and raced around to Austin's side of the table. "Oh my God, oh my God, are you hurt?" She checked his arms, his face, and then pulled his leg out from under the table hard enough that he winced when his knee cracked against the table leg.

"Amie," Jake roared. "What are you doing?"

She took a deep breath and asked Austin, "Are you hurt?" Her arms were all over him, checking him out.

"No," he replied, grabbing her hands to still them, "not

anymore. I've recovered."

She searched his face for a long moment and then let out a breath. "Damn good thing. Otherwise I would find out who hurt you and would make a special trip to see them," she declared in a threatening tone.

He gave her a kiss on the cheek and muttered, "I forgot how fearsome you are when you get riled."

"You better believe it," she snapped. "Now what's this about a prosthetic?"

He shrugged. "My leg."

She looked down at his jean-covered leg and asked forcefully, "How bad was it?"

"I'm walking. I'm alive. I'm doing fine," he stated. "I've come to terms with it, so all you need to know is that I'm okay."

"But you walked in here," she stated in confusion.

"Yes, that's what happens when you get prosthetics, particularly good ones."

"I think I've heard something about that woman," Jake shared, frowning. He shook his head, muttering, "I'll be damned if I know why."

"Kat's certainly made a name for herself. If you know anybody who has prosthetics," Austin noted, "she is the person to contact for custom work."

Jake nodded but stared off into the distance, still frowning. "I used to know a guy named Badger."

At that, Austin chuckled. "That's her husband."

He stared at him, his eyebrows popping up. "Seriously?"

Austin nodded. "Yes, the two of them are together and have a couple kids. Badger also has prosthetics, and Kat was born with a leg that never quite worked and never grew. At some point in time, her doctors and her parents decided to surgically remove it because it was more of a hindrance than a help, and that's how her love affair with prosthetics was born."

"Oh my," Amie whispered, as she stared at him, "that must have been hard."

"I think for Kat it was much harder to have a shorter leg drag around behind her that she couldn't use," he clarified. "She's an amazing person."

Austin realized that Rox hadn't said a word, but that was fine with him. If she couldn't handle a prosthetic, she sure as hell couldn't handle the nightmares that kept him up in the middle of the night either.

When the conversation turned back to the ranch and any other question he could ask to deflect the interest from him, Austin finally stood up and noted, "It was a long drive."

Amie bounced to her feet. "Come on. I'll help you get settled."

As she turned to head toward the stairs, Austin shook his head and suggested, "I would really be fine to crash in the bunkhouse." He watched at Amie's back stiffened, but he shook his head. "It's probably for the best."

Then Amie turned to face him. With the fighting look that came into Amie's gaze, Austin knew he was in for a battle.

Behind him, Jake called out. "You might as well give it up, son. When she's got her mind made up, it doesn't matter what you say."

Austin winced and turned to face Jake. "You know it's for the best."

"I'm right here, you know," Rox declared, standing up from the table and glaring at the two of them. "You don't have to talk over me."

"It's not as if you were joining in on the conversation at the end," Austin replied smoothly, "so I wasn't expecting you to care."

She glared at him, looked over at Amie, and shook her head. "Do whatever you want to do."

Amie nodded. "I will," she declared, tilting her head up higher. "Don't you worry. I will." She stared at Austin. "Now, get going up the stairs and enough of your arguing."

He hid a smile as he followed the petite-sized boss of the house up the stairs to the spare bedroom. He stood here in the hallway and leaned against the doorjamb.

Amie said, "Now don't tell me it brings back painful memories because it also brings back sweet memories too."

"Sure, but it's also about everything else I lost."

She froze at that and slowly nodded. "Yes, it is, but it's up to you if you want to find what you lost."

"No," he countered. "I can't go through that again."

She smiled up at him. "I know that." As she walked to the door, she patted him on the shoulder. "I know that you need to come and go and do your own thing, but you should know that Charlie is still here, and he's looking for some exercise."

He stared at her in surprise. "I don't think that would be the same response Jake would give me."

"You don't mind anything those two have to say," Amie proclaimed firmly. "Charlie is mine, always has been, always will be, and he adored you."

That she used the past tense almost brought tears to Austin's eyes, but he nodded. "I need to spend some time out on the road."

"Anytime you need, I'll pack you a lunch, and do not let those two stop you from doing what you need to do."

He gave her a wry smile. "I won't let them stop me," he confirmed. "I'm here on behalf of the War Department, and it just would have made life easier and a lot simpler if I stayed in town and didn't have to deal with anything else."

"Not dealing with it is what got you into this trouble," she spat, poking him in the chest, "and that time has long gone past, so sit up, straighten up, and do what you need to do to turn your life around."

"My life is turned around," he pointed out, with a note of amusement. "Believe it or not, I'm quite happy with where I am at these days."

She turned to glare at him. "No, you're not," she argued. "Somebody who doesn't know you well might not see it, but I do. I know that you've convinced yourself that you can live like you are, and you absolutely can," she conceded, as she shook her head. "Yet that doesn't mean you have to, and it sure as hell doesn't mean that you should. Remember that you are with people who love you, even if their own tempers and hurt feelings are keeping them at bay for the moment. This … whatever it is … will go away in a wash," she stated, with a smile. And, with that, she was gone.

Austin took a few steps to the bed and crashed onto it, staring up at the ceiling. Out loud he wondered, "What the hell did you get me into, Kat?"

If Kat knew his history, both personal and naval—and chances are that she did—that's exactly why she sent him here, and that was a messed-up thing to do. Yet, in a way, he also understood. He'd fought confronting this issue over the past five years, but a moment of truth and understanding had also hit Austin as he had spoken with Kat. He really couldn't go forward until he cleaned up his past, and, even though he understood that, it just wasn't something that he wanted to do.

Hell, it wasn't something he figured he should have to do either, if he were honest. When he turned and picked up his phone, Rox was staring at him from the doorway. He raised an eyebrow. "Yes?" His tone was cool, polite, but distant.

Rox hesitated for a moment but relented. "Don't let Mom talk you into doing anything you don't want to do."

He froze at that and asked, "What do you mean by that?"

She shrugged. "She's obviously hoping we'll reconcile."

He laughed. "The day for that is long gone."

She sent him a look he couldn't quite read, then turned and walked away, leaving him wondering if he'd just done something wrong. But, as far as he was concerned, there was no going back, not after all this time. And there sure as hell was no going back to the life that he'd had before with Rox.

Was she still dynamite, in and out of bed?

Probably.

Was she still somebody he would love forever?

Yes, but that didn't mean he could live *with* her or that he was interested in even trying anymore. As he'd already pointed out, that time had passed.

CHAPTER 3

R OX SLOWLY WALKED back down the stairs, opened the front porch door, and stepped outside, taking several deep breaths. Knowing it would take a whole lot more than that to calm her stomach and to get some semblance of order back in her head, she headed over to the barn. As soon as she stepped inside, she heard Charlie raising hell. He always seemed to sense when she was around.

She walked over to the huge chestnut gelding, stepping into the stall to wrap her arms around his neck and to just hold him close. He nickered softly against her hair. He'd always been the most sensitive and the most aware, the gentlest, and the most nonjudgmental of all the horses she'd fallen in love with over the years. She would save every animal on the planet if she could, which she wouldn't say about humans. It seemed as if animals never hurt each other anywhere near to the extent that people did.

She hoped that remained true with Cowboy. She knew full well the bigger wild animals in this area could have gotten the better of Cowboy, especially if he had been injured or was unconscious somewhere. Rox knew every dog had a survival instinct that kicked in, but especially a trained War Dog. So Cowboy would hunt for food and watering holes. The ranch supplied both. Still, Rox worried about Cowboy being struck down, muzzled, in a trap, or down a ravine. Then how would he get the water and the food that he needed? If he couldn't move, how would he defend himself?

After several long moments, she started the chores, finding peace and solace in the everyday parts of her world, something that she desperately needed to calm herself down. In her heart, she hadn't expected to ever really see Austin again, and yet she'd put things in motion that would bring him back to her, if at all possible. When he had shown up, she didn't even know what to think, didn't know how to act. She reverted to a self-conscious teenager all over again, a teen who wasn't welcome to be part of the equation when it came to Austin.

It was such a horrible feeling.

Her mother had absolutely adored Austin, and her father had too. The breakup had been devastating for the whole family, and more so because Rox didn't have any good reason for what she'd done. She did have a reason, but being a stupid young woman didn't come across as a particularly good excuse, not when her father stared at her in shock, trying to take in what she'd just done.

It had taken a lot of time for Dad to ease back and to forgive her for her part in it all. Her mother had forgiven her first, but had told her that sometimes things happened and that they just needed time to work themselves out.

Her father hadn't been anywhere near as positive about her situation, which allowed her to see part of his character, to see how he would have handled it if her mom had done that to her dad. Which, of course, didn't make Rox feel any better, but her mom had at least been much more understanding.

The fact that the ensuing five years had gone by and that

nobody suggested a divorce had helped, yet Rox lived in constant fear that it would be the next thing that came in the mail for her. Then to come home and to find Austin here, sitting at her kitchen table, had been a heart-wrenching moment.

She moved through the barn, her steps calm, easy, and steady. She'd done this for years, decades even. She had been born here, had grown up here, had been married here, had lived here with her husband, and then had separated here. She stopped several times and stared out at the world around her. After a heavy sigh, she went back to work. No answers were to be found here. All she was really looking for—and she stopped at that because she realized that she was seeking forgiveness. She wasn't even sure that was attainable now, but, if she could somehow find that through Austin's visit, as hard as it would be, it would at least allow her to move on, something that she hadn't managed to do on her own.

Her mother never seemed to expect Rox to move on, which was another strange thing. Her mom appeared to be waiting for Austin to come home again. When he did, it somehow seemed as if they hadn't missed a day. It was the strangest feeling to see Austin here, talking with her mom and dad, as if that were the most normal thing to do. Even her dad seemed to have thawed somewhat. His only comment over the years was that the boy was taking his sweet time, and Rox realized, to some extent, that her father too had hoped Austin would return. She had as well for the longest time, until she realized he had taken her at her word and had left … for good.

When she finished her chores, she walked back to Charlie, gave him another big hug, picked up the curry brush, and started working on his coat. The one thing there wasn't enough of was brushing these animals. She certainly wasn't in the state of mind to go to bed anytime soon, particularly knowing that Austin had his own room up there, just down the hall from her.

It was too close.

When they were dating, Rox used to sneak into the bunkhouse to visit Austin, to spend the night if no other ranch hands were around, and then to sneak back into her own room in the main house, knowing full well that her parents knew what was going on. It had been sheer luck that had Austin wanting to leave town, his namesake, to spend a long leave from the navy that he had coming to him by taking a summer gig as a ranch hand. He was waiting for his next navy assignment, and this change of pace was just what he thought he needed.

When they got married, there had been nobody happier than her mom and dad, and everybody had been absolutely sure that this would be a marriage that lasted forever. Rox too. And it would have lasted forever if Rox hadn't been such an idiot. Repeating that same damn negativity over and over back then had led to Rox going to therapy on the sly because she didn't want anybody to know.

Now that she no longer saw the shrink, Rox just kept talking to Charlie, telling him that he would go out in the fields again soon and that somebody he absolutely loved was back. Nobody knew for how long, but Austin was here now, and Charlie would surely have the benefit of Austin's presence.

Charlie nickered several times, a slow, gentle rolling of muscles pushing air up through that long beautiful neck of his, such a comforting, cozy sound that brought back memories all over again.

Rox didn't know when it started, but her tears started to pour, and she had no way to stop them. She just bowed her head against Charlie's huge back and let them fly. It didn't last long, but it was intense. By the time the flood stopped, she was drained, completely exhausted, her whole body feeling the grief all over again. Grief over what she'd done and knowing she had destroyed something precious and irreplaceable. Now here she was, a whole lot older, a whole lot wiser, and yet, in many ways—specifically on this issue— still not stronger.

She gave Charlie a big hug, wiped her face, and whispered, "Thanks, buddy. You're right. I did need that."

She gave him an extra hug, then slipped out of the barn and into the darkness of the night. She wasn't going up to her room yet. The thought of meeting Austin in the hallway, looking like she did, was wholly unacceptable, so that wasn't happening. She sat quietly in the dark, as her world fell apart, just trying to observe everything going on and hoping for some closure. … Maybe that's all she wanted.

She knew that was a lie, but, hey, if that's what she could get, she would take it because that was something she craved. She really needed a way to move on, to move forward, to find peace, and, if that was on the table, then she would do anything she could to get it.

Just as she got up to walk back into the house and to head up to her room, she thought she heard a noise off in the distance. She stared at the other side of the ranch, seeing the flickering lights ever-so-faintly in the distance. She frowned, opened up the front door to the house and called out to her father. He rumbled forward, and she motioned out into the distance.

He started swearing. "What the hell now?" he muttered.

"I'm taking the boys to check this out. You go in and look after your mother."

And, with that, he was gone, delegating Rox once again to the role of a little woman, but one with the job most precious to Jake, which was protecting her mother's life, and yet this wasn't a job of protection. It could be cattle rustlers out there. It could be nothing. It could be a fire starting off in the distance, but the bottom line was that everybody had a role in this world, and Rox's was to keep the home fires burning, making sure her very special and precious mother was okay.

And, with that, Rox headed inside, calling out to her mother.

AUSTIN HAD STEPPED out of the barn, after hearing the sobs inside, his heart twisting with regret, anguish, and anger. It's not as if he'd brought this on; that was all her. He pinched the bridge of his nose and swore under his breath. He'd forced himself to *not* contact her years ago, so hurt and devastated by everything that she'd said back then, which he recited whenever he thought of coming back to her. Recalling her words steeled him, so he'd walked and just kept on walking.

It's easy to forget when out on a mission, easy to just focus on the things that you wanted to remember, and it was never all about the good things. When times were tough, it was usually the rotten things that helped you to reinforce your stance and your beliefs. It never really did him any good, but, hey, he'd gone from one mission to another after that, refusing to ever step back home again. It had been hard at first, but, when the years rolled along, it became easier to reinforce the fact that he had nothing at home for him anyway.

He hadn't even come back for his stuff. He'd slipped out of the house pretty quickly after she'd told him to go and to never come back. So he had left their bedroom, just to go for a walk. He walked the fence, with one of the dogs, Chester, at his side, half to keep him out of trouble and half to ensure he didn't do something he wasn't allowed to do. The dogs were incredibly protective and always had been. Austin had always been very much a dog person, and, hell, he was also a horse person. He was an animal lover in general.

His ruminations of the past were interrupted as Austin thought he heard some noises coming from the barn. People were suddenly up and heading out to take a look at something. He didn't have any wheels capable to take on the ranch lands or a mount, so no way he could catch up with them. Yet, as he walked in that direction, somebody came up behind him. He stood still, waiting for the recognition.

Jake called out, "The least you can do is get on a damn horse and help."

"If I had known there was a problem, I would have," Austin replied in a calm tone.

Jake asked, "Did you hear anything out here?"

"No, I was just coming to investigate an odd sound, when I heard you guys."

"You won't get far without something under you," Jake noted in a hard tone. "Either grab a four-wheeler or go saddle up, but this isn't a time to not be partaking." Jake took off, galloping his horse into the dark.

Austin laughed. So typical of the man. Jake was all about getting out there and doing what needed to be done and doing it fast before anybody else got there. It wasn't a bad attitude, particularly if crap was going on that you needed to take care of. Austin headed back to the barn and found Charlie, who recognized him and started nickering.

He quickly saddled him up, grabbing the closest saddle, not even knowing whose it was or if somebody was particular about this one. Jumping up into the saddle, Austin and Charlie took off after the others. Austin was never one to be left behind and wanted to be in the action at all times. As he raced over the ground, he smiled with joy, completely forgetting about his prosthetic, just getting up and moving out fast, not missing a beat. That freedom and the sense of recognition that he really could still do this was so absolutely stunning that he just wanted to laugh out loud.

Even as he came abreast of Jake and one of the ranch hands that he didn't recognize, Jake looked over at him and nodded. "Glad to see it didn't hold you back."

Austin figured he meant the injury, but he wasn't sure, so he just nodded and replied, "I don't hold back easily."

"No, maybe not," Jake muttered, "but the shit women can do will turn your guts inside out. I know Rox tossed you out, like some discarded piece of meat. Don't ever let anybody do that to you. Not even my daughter. You should have more self-respect than that."

"Wasn't planning on it."

Jake snorted. "Too late, you already did."

"Maybe," Austin conceded, "but I'm not the same person I was before."

"That's a damn good thing," Jake stated, "but you've also got to remember that neither is she." And, with that, he nudged his horse to a higher speed and tore off toward whatever was causing chaos up ahead.

Austin followed quickly behind, and he had the ranch hand right with him. As they came to a clearing, they found vehicles tearing off into the distance, looking to have just been joyriding on Jake's land.

Jake raced up behind them, trying to take photos or something along that line, with the other ranch hand coming up behind him. Seeing the direction the vehicles took, Austin veered off, heading toward the road to intercept them. He couldn't stop them, not on a horse, but, if he could get close enough to identify them in any way, that would be a different story. This shit would never go down well, not where animals were involved, livestock, especially not when the brush was as dry as hell, and a fire could start without anybody even thinking about it.

As soon as Austin cut through the brush and kept on going, he just gave Charlie his head, knowing that the horse would know his way far better than anybody else. It didn't take long before he came to an opening to see the vehicles crash through the brush, heading directly for him. Charlie reared off to the side, and Austin quickly took photos of a modified pickup truck, lifted, with huge tires underneath. It generally looked like a kid's toy that had been souped-up, rather than anybody serious about riding off-road. Austin figured it was just some locals out having fun, probably drunk and high as a kite, but still dangerous as hell.

He couldn't keep up the pace, and, laughing and screaming at him, the driver of the vehicle took off. But Austin had enough photos to identify the vehicle. Plus, he thought he recognized who was inside, and that wouldn't make Austin or anybody else happy.

Unfortunately it looked to be Amie's son.

CHAPTER 4

ROX STOOD ON the porch, tapping her foot impatiently. When Jake and Austin finally came in from the barn, she barked, "Well?"

"What the hell was that?" Glaring, her father brushed past her and went inside, as she turned and stared in astonishment. That didn't bode well.

With Jake in the house, she watched Austin moving toward her at a rapid pace. She stepped aside to let him in, and, as he went by, she whispered, "What the hell is going on?"

"Not exactly sure, but it wasn't good." He headed in toward the kitchen, with her trailing behind.

"What was it?" she snapped. She glared at Austin. "Come on. Give me a straight answer."

He shrugged. "I saw the driver, didn't recognize him. … It was dark, with only the lights of the vehicle and their spotlights and my phone's flash camera, but"—he turned to face Jake and Amie—"I think Chris was in the passenger seat."

Immediately Rox's heart stopped. She stared at Amie, then at Jake, as she turned back to Austin. "You have to be wrong."

He replied in a tight tone of voice, "I wish I was wrong, but all I can tell you is what I saw, and it looked to be

Chris." He pulled out his phone and started bringing up the photographs.

Rox snatched the phone from his hand and studied the pictures, her heart sinking. She looked over to see her mom staring at her, with fear in her eyes, but Rox nodded slowly. "Shit, it does look to be Chris."

Her mom closed her eyes and leaned back on the counter for support, as if everything in her world had just collapsed. She turned to Austin. "Was anyone else with him?"

Austin shrugged. "You can't really see from the photos, but he had at least one if not two other people with him." She just bit her bottom lip and nodded. "I gather things have gotten way worse?" Austin asked her.

"Oh yeah, way worse, not that it was ever very good to begin with."

Austin didn't know the whole story. Only that Chris was Amie's son, not Jake's.

Even as siblings growing up together, Rox and Chris used to get along so well for many, many years, until the more recent ones. She had tried to talk to Chris several times, but it had always turned into a mockery, siccing his friends on her, calling her the poor little rich girl. Chris had changed, never really adapting past the point of learning that he would inherit a 25 percent share of ownership in the ranch. That had broken Rox's heart to see him so angry all the time because the last thing Rox wanted was to come between Chris and his mother. For Amie, he was still her firstborn, a child she absolutely adored, but one who appeared to have no love for his mother at all.

Rox had wanted to kick Chris's butt so many times just for mistreating Amie, for not loving the wonderful mother he had, yet Rox could not do anything with him, not now, not after the *inherit* talk Jake had had with Chris. He was stubborn, he was arrogant, and he was hurting and lashing out. If she understood one thing, it was hurting. She walked over and wrapped her arms around her mother and held her close.

Amie shook with pain, frustration, and anger, but mostly hurt.

Rox held her close and murmured, "It'll be okay."

Amie just shook her head, then looked at her. "You know it won't be okay. This won't end well for anybody," she murmured.

At that, Rox nodded. "I'm afraid so too," she admitted, "but I'm not sure what else we can do. Somehow we have to talk to Chris."

"We just can't get through to him," Amie stated in frustration. "You think I haven't tried?" She pushed back her hair and stepped out of her daughter's reach, always needing to be in control, trying so hard to make everything perfect in the world around her. When somebody didn't conform and refused to follow suit it, it broke all the molds of everything that Amie had always done for them. It hurt Rox to see her mother in so much pain. She turned back to Jake and asked, "Ideas?"

He shook his head. "Nope. I'm hamstrung. If it wasn't for your mother, I would have called the cops a long time ago."

Austin spoke up, resolute and firm. "You'll have to now, Jake." Amie turned on him with a harsh gasp, and he shook his head. "You and I both know that the time for being nice is long over. I don't know how far Chris has gone off the reservation doing crap like this," he pointed out, "but it is definitely not something you can allow him to continue to do. He'll just get into more and more trouble. Joyriding is one thing, but lighting fires is another," he declared, staring Amie right in her eyes. "He's deliberately trying to hurt you. I don't know any way forward on that, but he obviously needs some help—or at least some new friends."

"He definitely needs new friends," Amie agreed, shaking her head. "He's only thirty."

Austin stared at her. "Thirty? Did you say *only thirty?*"

Amie winced and then nodded. "I know, in your world, thirty is a man."

"In anybody's world," he stated, his tone hard. "Thirty is a man, and in this case it's a man-size problem that needs to be fixed."

"I don't know how to fix it," Amie shared simply. "I've tried talking to him, and he just won't listen. He's angry."

"About what?"

"About the ranch," Jake said, followed by a harsh grunt. "I offered him a share—25 percent—and a working relationship as part of the ranch operation. Honestly, it never occurred to me that he wouldn't want that or wouldn't want to stay and work together, but he basically laughed and threw it in my face. He doesn't want any part of it."

"So, what does he want?" Austin asked.

"He wants all of it. Yet Rox is my daughter, related by blood," he stated, "and I will not pass down the family legacy, generations upon generations to Chris, not without Rox being a part of it, and she would get the larger share at that," he added firmly. "Otherwise it'll go back to my cousin."

Silence followed his words, and Austin knew that had been an issue prior to his separation from Rox. It had never been an issue for Austin. It would obviously be Rox's place—as a family legacy, of course it was. He had also expected to eventually stay and work the land with her. Back then he just hadn't realized that, for Rox, the *eventually* was to be *immediately*, as far as she was concerned.

Austin nodded. "Of course Chris didn't like the reality of your offer when he was expecting a handout, where his inheritance would cost Rox hers."

"Exactly. His biological father is out there in the world and isn't giving him shit, so ..." Jake puffed up his cheeks and let out a sigh. "Chris is holding it against me that I'm not his natural father and that I won't just hand over my family's legacy to him."

"He's also never worked the ranch," Rox pointed out. "He doesn't want to work here. He doesn't want to be part of it, and, when Dad told him that he could live and work here, Chris got angry and took off."

Austin frowned at that. "I don't remember him as being that angry before."

She shook her head. "He wasn't, but it happened somewhere around the same time as we broke up," she admitted, "but I'm not sure what started it. I just know that Chris made a point of making sure that he's the one in control, and the rest of us really have no say. He just bounces in and bounces out, upsets Mom, and goes on about his day, a smile on his face, as if that makes him the happiest man ever."

"So, he's still lashing out at you then," Austin noted, turning to look at Amie.

She had one fist up against her mouth, as if to hold back an inner scream, something he understood full well. He walked over, wrapped her up in his arms, and just let her rock against him. "I'm sorry." He turned and looked at Jake.

"Are you thinking this is the only issue, or is something else going on?"

"Something else is going on," he confirmed, with a shake of his head, "and it has to do with his girlfriend."

"Ex-girlfriend," Rox clarified.

Jake asked Austin, "Remember Danny, one ranch over? He has a daughter, Samantha. Do you remember her?"

He shrugged. "Vaguely, yes."

"Danny didn't approve of Chris dating Samantha and more or less kicked Chris off his place. He'd caught him in her bed a couple times, had some strong words, and kicked him out of the house. He hasn't been allowed back and isn't allowed to date Samantha anymore."

Austin thought about that for a long moment and then nodded. "She's a bit younger, isn't she?"

"Yeah, quite a few years younger, if truth be told," Jake confirmed. "I think she's four or five years younger than you, isn't she?" he asked, turning to look at Rox.

"Seven years younger than me. She's eighteen," she shared, "and she's always been a handful. So, it's not necessarily all Chris's fault."

Amie shook her head. "No, it's not all his fault, but I'm sure, from Chris's perspective, once again he wasn't enough, and nobody was there for him."

Austin sighed. "So, basically Chris had a chip on his shoulder already, then got into trouble with a young girl whose father didn't approve, and that was it?"

"Pretty much," Jake noted, "and now we have a very angry young man."

"Who apparently has money," Austin broke in, "if that set of wheels was anything to go by."

"I think that truck is his buddy's. Chris only works part-time at the mechanic's shop," Jake said cautiously. "I'm not sure if that's a good thing for him or not, but at least it's solid work, and it does keep him off the streets—at least some hours of the day."

"Where is he living?" Austin asked.

"Above the gas station. Carmichael gave him a place when he was there last time."

"That's a good thing then because it could be worse."

"It could be, but another kid stays there as well. As far as I know, that kid is pretty heavily into drugs, and I figure the fancy truck was probably his."

"Ah, and that'll just make Chris even angrier because an awful lot of kids around here have big stakes in large established ranches, and everybody knows everybody else's business. So the details of the families and how the money will go is fairly common knowledge. So, if you were born into a family like this, generally you'll stay with a family like this."

"In most cases, yes," Jake conceded, with a nod. "I'm not doing anything different by trying to keep my own ranch intact," he declared. "I know an awful lot of people might judge me for it, but I didn't kick Chris out. I offered him a place. He just doesn't get to have it all." Jake shrugged. "None of us do, and that's just life."

AUSTIN WOKE THE next morning bright and early. He got out of bed, had a quick shower in the nearby bathroom, then headed downstairs to the kitchen. He wasn't exactly sure how to start his day, but he needed to get started on finding the War Dog, one way or another, and that meant going to town to make a few inquiries. An ugly suspicion was already in the back of his head, but it would be a tough thing to even consider. Last night's scenario had opened up a whole pile of other options in terms of Cowboy, the War Dog. As much as Austin didn't want to contemplate those options, there really wasn't a whole lot of choice when it came right down to it.

As he walked into the kitchen, he found Amie industriously frying up what looked to be pounds of bacon. He smiled and muttered, "That brings back memories."

"Good," she replied, without turning around. "I'm glad at least some of your memories are good."

"Lots of my memories are good," he murmured, studying her, aware that she didn't sound great, as if she were at a breaking point. "I gather you didn't get any sleep."

She shook her head. "No, but that's okay. I'll have a nap later today."

And that was likely a lie too, but he let it go because she was obviously still struggling with last night's scenario. "Do you ever see him at all?"

"No," she whispered. "He doesn't come around anymore."

"What about you? Do you go into town at all?"

"Not as often as I used to, and certainly not when he's with that group."

"Are you afraid of him?"

She turned to face Austin. "I don't think so, but I'm not so sure I would give his friends the same pass."

"Okay." Austin admired the way that she broke that out. "That's a good point. So, the others are not great for him, I gather?"

"No," she agreed, her tone sharp, "they're not a good influence at all."

Austin had to smile because he wasn't sure any mother ever thought anybody was a good influence on their children. However, with an already troubled son like Chris, she could be right. "I will head into town to talk to him."

She froze and then turned around in shock. "Why?"

"Because I need to talk to him, just for my own peace of mind."

She shook her head. "It'll just make things worse."

"I don't see how," Austin stated. "It must be pretty bad already if a conversation will make things worse. I used to get along with him, but I highly doubt he has any memories of me."

"He does remember you because we were all upset when you left," Amie replied, glancing around to see if her daughter was here.

"Right, and how did Chris take it?"

"He just laughed and said that Rox messed up."

Austin smiled. "I always knew I liked Chris."

She looked at him and laughed. It was awkward and sad, but it was a laugh. "He wasn't the only one to tell her that," she added. "We were all pretty upset about it."

He ignored that subject. "So last night Jake talked about Chris living above a gas station. So whereabouts is that?"

She nodded. "I don't know if you remember, but Carmichael has a gas station down just off the main street. You know, around the corner from Rubie's."

"Has Rubie's still got pie?" he asked, frowning as he remembered the name.

Amie laughed. "Yes, Rubie's still has the best pie in town, … outside of mine, of course," she added.

"Yours is absolutely phenomenal," Austin confirmed, "but I'm not against going in and seeing if theirs is still good."

She shook her head. "You go do you," she muttered. "I'm not sure I have the strength to do anything about any of this."

"Not sure that you have to either," Austin noted. "Let me talk to Chris and see what he has to say for himself."

"Do you think he'll even recognize you?" she asked him.

"I don't know, but it's a really good opening for me because I sure as hell recognized him in that truck last night," he declared, with a smile. He poured himself some coffee and sat down at the table. "Is Jake gone?"

"Not yet. He's out in the barn, setting up the day's work, then wants to take a look where Chris was joy-riding to ensure that nothing was damaged, that none of the animals were injured out there."

"Yeah, that would be a good thing," Austin agreed, his tone hardening. "My talk would be a whole lot different if I thought Chris had hurt any of the cows."

"There are also calves, and he likes to make them run," she shared bitterly. "I didn't raise that boy to do that. I just don't know what went wrong."

"That's why I'm curious. I want to understand what went wrong. As Jake mentioned, if that talk of Chris's inheritance is all there is to it, then Chris has got to think again because life doesn't hand you ranches just because that's what you want."

She glanced nervously around. "And I didn't tell him about his inheritance either," she admitted, "so it would have blindsided him. It didn't even occur to me. I knew that Jake would keep Chris involved in the ranch to some degree. I just didn't think Chris was so gung-ho about the ranch. It's not his thing. Never really has been. He's much happier at the mechanic's shop, I hear."

"Sounds as if it was probably an all-or-nothing deal in Chris's mind somehow. It's not your fault."

"Isn't it?" she whispered, her shoulders hunching. "It sure feels like it is."

"That's human nature," he pointed out, "but Chris was offered a sweet deal, with a place here, to live and to work, with a share in the whole ranch."

"But it also meant working the ranch, and that's not ever been something Chris was willing to do. All he ever wanted was the money that comes with it."

"That's too bad, isn't it?" Austin muttered, staring at her. "We all want things we can't have, but that doesn't mean we can just turn around and take from others because we don't like the options." Austin frowned, as Amie looked older than he remembered.

She continued. "I've got to admit, since you left, there's been some pretty rough days."

He winced at that. "I'm sorry," he murmured. "And I'm sorry for any of the extra pain I caused you."

She smiled. "It wasn't your fault. I'm sorry you thought you had to leave, but I get it. I'm married too, and not all of it is easy, and ultimatums? … They just make everything way worse," she stated. "My daughter had a lot of growing up to do, but I will tell you this. She has done a ton of growing up in the meantime."

"Good." Austin nodded. "That should make her all the happier in the end."

Amie sighed, looked at him, and said, "If you do talk to Chris, I know you don't want to tell him that I love him, but I really do."

"Of course you do," he said. "He's your son, but he's also a flawed human being, like all of us, and he's messing up big-time, and that crap has got to stop."

"But if you go in there like that, it'll likely piss him right off, and he'll get even angrier, and then he'll be out here to cause all kinds of trouble," she whispered. "I don't think I can handle that."

"You'll handle it," he declared, "just like you've handled everything else, with grace, compassion, and love. If he's not willing to accept any of Jake's generosity or your love or Rox's friendship, you can't do anything about it, except to give him the space to deal with his own choices. ... However, if he's breaking the law, he will have to pay for that."

She studied him for a moment and asked, "Ever think about going into law enforcement?"

He laughed. "I thought about it a lot, trying to figure out what I'm doing with my life now," he admitted, "but I can't say I've come up with any firm answers."

"I don't quite understand," she said. "Aren't you working for the War Department?"

He nodded. "Yeah, but this will be the only job I do for them."

"Oh. What will you do after that?"

"I need to figure that out, but I haven't gotten there just yet. I'm looking at options right now. I can always sign up for a desk job."

"I can't imagine you behind a desk," she muttered, her eyes widening.

"Not sure I can either, but we all can do things we didn't think we could," he replied. "It depends on the options and what is really important to you."

She nodded slowly. "I hear you there," she murmured, "and I really appreciate what you're doing here."

"I'm not doing anything yet," he pointed out, with a

smile. "I'm here looking for a War Dog that's in desperate need of some help, apparently. Other than that, I am heading home afterward."

Amie winced. "That is your choice, but I still think you need to know that she's not the same person."

"Good," he noted, "and neither am I." With that, he dug in to a large plate of breakfast, looking up a few minutes later as Rox walked in. He glanced at her and asked, "Sleep well?"

She hesitated, then nodded with a shrug. "Well enough," she muttered.

He smiled. "*Well enough*, considering your world has just been flipped?"

She gave him a wry smile. "Something like that, yeah."

"What do you know about your brother's friends?"

"Enough to know that they are not people I want to hang out with," she stated. "I think one had a record as a juvenile, but I don't know for sure." She waved her hand as she sat down to a full breakfast herself. "A fair bit of drugs and booze are involved with that bunch," she added, with a shrug. "Small towns, you know? You can get into trouble pretty quick."

"But not you," he noted, with a hint of amusement in his tone.

"Oh, I got into plenty of trouble," she admitted, "but you were always there to get me out of it."

He nodded. "I missed that stage with Chris."

"Yeah, he was older than me, so got out of high school before I graduated, but he spent a couple years going to a different school while living with his dad, then came back angry," she explained thoughtfully, as she looked over at Amie, who nodded.

"Chris really wanted to live with his father for a while," Amie confirmed.

Austin asked, "So … do you think Chris believes the reason why he's not getting the ranch for himself is about living with his father?"

"I don't know why he would even think that he could get the whole ranch. We've never hidden that from him," Rox declared, eyeing Austin. "I'm not getting the whole ranch either."

"What does that mean?" Austin asked.

Rox shrugged. "Chris was supposed to be part owner of it, but I don't think Dad will do that now. He can't trust Chris, and Dad doesn't want to risk the family property being sold for drug money or for money to escape this life. You have to be part of this life in order to be on the title as the owner."

"Right," Austin agreed, "and, once they're on the title, they have voting power."

"Exactly," she muttered, "and it would break my family's heart if I lost generations of history here because of that."

"Of course," he murmured, as he finished his breakfast.

She looked over at him and asked, "Do you need Charlie today? Are you heading out to see where Cowboy spent his last day here?"

"I will be in a little bit. First, I'll head into town really quick, touch base with my boss, then stop in and see your brother."

Her jaw dropped, and she stared at him. "Is that a good thing?"

"I don't know," he said, "but I sure as hell recognized him last night. That gives me an opening for a conversation, and I think it's well past time somebody talked to him."

"It's not your job," she warned.

"Yet the people who should have done it … didn't," he pointed out. "So who else will do it, if I don't?"

And, with that, he got up and walked out.

CHAPTER 5

ROX HEADED OFF to the barn to start the chores, knowing that she was late, already chastising herself for it.

As she walked into the barn, her father was there with Raul and Carlos. She listened in on the instructions for the day, then the two ranch hands took off.

Her father turned to her and asked, "What are you up to today?"

She raised an eyebrow. "The same thing as always. Nothing's changed." He frowned but didn't say anything, just staring off into the distance. "Nothing has changed, Dad," she reiterated. "Austin's here for a short while, and that doesn't impact me at all."

He nodded. "Maybe it should."

"Maybe it should, but it doesn't. He didn't come here for me. He came here for the War Dog, and he's made that very clear."

Jake's lips twitched. "I could make a comment about the way you're acting and how it relates to the female of the dog species."

She glared at him and then reluctantly smiled. "You could make a comment about that, and in many ways you would also be right. But call me whatever you like, it still doesn't change the fact that Austin didn't come here for me."

"No, but he probably doesn't even know if he's welcome to talk to you."

"He's never been afraid of talking to me before."

"Ah, but I think things are very different now, don't you?"

"Maybe," she nodded, "but it doesn't matter. I'm heading out to the west pasture to check the well and the cattle over there."

He nodded. "Good enough. I'll head back out to see how much damage Chris did last night."

She winced. "Okay. You go do that, and we'll touch base toward the end of the day."

"Keep your cell phone on you."

She didn't expect the sharpness to his tone. She turned to face him. "Are you expecting trouble?"

"I don't expect trouble," he stated, "but you never know what's going on with Chris."

"Right, I hear you. ... I'm just sorry that we haven't been able to reach him."

"You and me both," he muttered. "Do you feel it's unfair?"

"What, the ranch?" When he nodded, she shook her head. "No, of course not. It's not as if you cut him out. You gave him an opportunity to be a part of all this, even though he's not at all interested in it. Not really. I think he wants to do something else. This ranch was never his thing, and I don't particularly think he cares about this life."

"That was part of the problem for me too," her dad confirmed. "I always felt as if he didn't give a crap, and that was hard for me."

"Of course it was," she agreed, waving her hand. "Shit like this just twists people around—anything with money and inheritances. Still, these big properties require someone to run it."

"I know," he muttered, "and I thought you had somebody to help you, once I was gone."

"Yeah, I did too," she said, "and then I messed up."

He shrugged. "But that doesn't mean you have to keep messing up." And, with that, he disappeared.

She glared at the barn door, wondering if he really intended that the way it sounded. It sure came across as if he had, but she wasn't up for any interrogations or discussions on her strange marital status.

Separated, but not legally, and not divorced either. What the hell was she supposed to do about that? She didn't know. On the other hand, it wasn't today's issue, and she was heading off to deal with the more pressing issue because there was never any shortage of work on a ranch this size.

Her dad was right though. They needed to be prepared for anything. Chris was angry, and, while she didn't think he would hurt her or their mother, absolutely no way would Rox trust those friends of his. And depending on how her brother really felt, he might not have a problem with siccing them on Rox, and that wasn't something she wanted to deal with.

She quickly saddled up and headed off, calling two of the dogs with her. Bonner and Chico were the ones that generally traveled with her, and pretty quickly they settled into a steady gait, heading out past the back porch. If she could have driven, she would have, but this was territory that was much better covered on horseback.

This wasn't the kind of a place where you could ignore any of these pastures for long. There was always some trouble with animals or something. Plus, she was always on the lookout for Cowboy. Yet, with each passing day, her hope died a little bit more.

They didn't have too many predators here, but they did have a few, and that was always something she had to be aware of. She loved animals, all animals, but when it came to a predator taking down one of her own animals, she would end that fight with a single bullet. She patted the rifle that she kept cross-tied in front of her on her saddle, knowing full well that she'd had to use it a few times, and she probably would again. So far, she'd been blessed, and it had always been something that she could deal with fairly easily. Yet she also knew that there would be times when it wouldn't be that way at all. There just couldn't be a safety net around her all the time.

She'd lost one dog already to a renegade mountain lion, and here she was with two at her side at all times, just in case. She said a little prayer for Cowboy. Today was a beautiful morning, and it didn't take long for her to relax a bit as she settled into an easy lope. The horse had picked up on her mood the minute she got on, so it was important for Rox to destress as much as she could while riding. It was much easier on all of them at the end of the day. It took an hour to get where she needed to go, and from there, she headed on around the fence, coming up on the section at the back.

She wandered around the outside edge of the cattle. They kept an eye on her as she moved, but she was a sight that they were used to seeing, an area of life they were used to dealing with. Therefore, her presence didn't cause any reaction from them. She moved slowly and calmly, with Chico and Bonner always near her side, following her orders.

She checked the water and made sure everything was

fine. A creek was off to the side, and she walked on through, checking on the yearlings as she headed up on the other side and moved over to another pasture. It was a route that they did weekly, sometimes every couple days, depending on the weather. If it was dry, she always had to check on the water. The droughts were the deadliest in these places, but everything today was calm and as it should be.

By the time she turned back and made her way around the fence line and down again, she started to feel pretty good, even relaxed and happy. This was her life and had been all she ever wanted. She had always wanted to be a part of this, to be a part of something bigger than her, something special, and this ranch was absolutely special. She never understood her brother's disdain for this life but was pretty darn sure it had more to do with the fact that he didn't want to be associated with anything that had to do with her. They normally got along well, and she thought Chris got along well with Jake, up until the issue of the ranch inheritance had come up. Chris was just proud and entitled enough to cause trouble for no reason, and that was just a constant irritant to their mother.

As she came up on the other side, she saw the highway off in the distance, checked that everything was well and kept on going. At this rate, she would end up home for lunch, something that she rarely managed to do. She laughed at the idea because the minute she even thought that, something was bound to go wrong. Sure enough, when she got around to the next pasture a few miles over, she found one of the calves struggling in the mud.

She managed to rope him and to pull him back out again, then hopped down to check on him and cleaned him up a little bit, until he got back up on his feet, bawling for his mother. The cow came running, and Rox barely got back up on her horse and out of the way before the angry mama charged. Rox quickly drew back out of reach and sat here, staring as the cow checked out the muddy calf.

"I know we're all hypervigilant when it comes to our offspring," she murmured to the cow, "but I just saved your baby's sorry ass. You know that, right?"

The cow didn't care one bit, so Rox went about her business and rode off, continuing to check pastures. She was coming alongside the highway again when she heard a honk from a distance away. She turned to see a strange vehicle, then realized it was Austin. She slowed down and waited until he pulled close enough and stopped.

He leaned through the window and asked her, "Everything okay?"

Her eyebrows shot up, and she nodded. "Yeah. Why?"

"Just checking." He shrugged.

"Did you talk to my brother?"

He nodded. "I tried." Then he shook his head. "He wouldn't come out and talk to me, but I'll go back in this afternoon. I did connect with my boss, so I wondered if you're up for taking a trip back out to where Cowboy was that whole day before he went missing that night or the next morning."

She frowned at that but then nodded. "Yes, we can do that." She checked her watch. "I'll meet you back at the ranch."

"Good enough. I'll be back in twenty."

"I'll be a bit longer than you," she muttered, then quickly turned and headed back cross-country.

"No worries," he replied.

She might make it before him, but it wasn't worth pushing Charlie for something like that. That was another thing that Chris never understood. He just didn't have a knack for animals, or equipment, or even a knack or feel for the land. Maybe in a way he was a fish out of water here, but, even still, it never really occurred to her that he would hate the ranch so much that he would actively work to destroy it.

She didn't know whether that was anger or something deeper, but the fact of the matter was that Chris was not the man she used to know, and, while it was not terrifying, it was definitely not something she was comfortable with. They'd had so much fun growing up together, and now it had somehow become something completely different. Something had changed him. She groaned as she headed back to the barn, then unsaddled Charlie and headed inside.

After eating lunch, she and Austin were about to head out to trace Cowboy's last day, when Austin motioned at her. "I can ride Charlie if you want," he offered.

"He's already been out all morning," she shared, "so it might be best to take one of the others."

Austin didn't say anything and just nodded.

"Surely he should be okay to go back out again, shouldn't he?" Amie asked, looking between the two of them.

"Maybe so, but there's no point in pushing him when we could be out for quite a while today, and we have other horses that could use the time riding anyway. We're heading to retrace Cowboy's last day before he disappeared."

"Right." Amie frowned, then nodded.

Rox continued. "It's probably better to leave Charlie here anyway."

"Why is that?" Amie asked.

"Because he was the one I was riding as we took Cowboy

around the ranch," Rox murmured, "and it seems as if, in a way, whatever happened that day affected Charlie somehow. He gets quite antsy any time we get near that certain pasture."

Austin stared at her for a long moment. "In that case, … maybe we should take him, see what that's about."

She shook her head. "No, at least not this time. If I'd realized you wanted to go out on Charlie, I wouldn't have taken him this morning." Austin just nodded and didn't say anything, but she could tell he didn't like her answer. "It's not as if Charlie will tell us much," she pointed out.

He grimaced and tilted his head. "I think you're wrong there. Charlie probably has a hell of a good idea exactly what went on, but I won't argue with you. That's a no-win situation for me."

Amie hid her smile as she handed them food for the trip. "Seeing as you'll be gone for a while, take some supplies."

"We've got supplies," Rox replied, yet took the food her mother handed to her. Rox headed out to the barn and saddled up two other horses. Austin joined her and asked which one he should take, and she pointed to one of the new geldings they had.

"As long as you've kept up your riding skills," she warned, "because he's not the most experienced horse with a rider."

Austin shrugged. "Haven't ridden much in a while, but there wasn't anything I couldn't ride, back in the day."

"You're not back in the day anymore," she stated. "You're older and broken." And, with that remark, she swung up onto her horse and headed to the gate. It was probably poor form on her part, but she also meant it. If he wasn't capable of doing the ride, she didn't want him out there dealing with what they could potentially find. It was also a long run, and if he wasn't fit and in shape, she needed to know before they headed out.

When she turned, he was already up on the horse and moving toward her. She checked his gait and then nodded. It didn't appear that he'd suffered anything major.

He passed through the gate before her, looking back at her. "I get that was a dig for my benefit, and I'm sure you may be thrilled that I came back *broken*," he replied, deliberately using her word, "but, just for the record, there isn't anything I could do before that I can't do now."

And, with that, leaving her ashamed at the words she had used, he took off in the direction they needed to go. They rode silently together for the longest time, and, when they finally got closer, she pulled off to the side and pointed. "I thought I saw him here one day."

He stopped and frowned at her. "What do you mean?"

"When I was out here a few days after Cowboy went missing, I thought I saw him right here."

"Did he respond to your call?"

She shook her head. "I'm not sure if he even could though. I just saw him from a distance, and I didn't get a good look before he was gone, but … it almost seemed as if maybe he was tethered somehow, maybe on a leash or something."

He frowned at her and asked, "So, you really don't know who has Cowboy, or you just don't want to admit who has him?"

She glared at him. "I don't know who has him," she snapped, "and I really don't like the way you're thinking about it."

"Come on, Rox. How could I not? After that whole joy-riding deal last night, the person who comes to mind is Chris."

"I know that," she snapped in exasperation, "and I'm sure that everybody else has probably thought about that too. But … what would his motive be?"

"To hurt you," he stated.

She opened her mouth, closed it, then muttered, "It would be pretty sad if that's all he cares about in life right now."

"If he's angry, and, from what I saw out here, he's an extremely angry man," Austin pointed out. "He's not thinking straight and, if he's got friends egging him on, that makes it far worse and opens the door for a lot more trouble."

"I know it's worse," she agreed, her breath coming out in a harsh groan. "He's been so angry at Mom since he came back from his time at his dad's, and I just don't know how to handle it."

"It's not for you to handle. It's for Chris to handle, and also for your mom, to some degree. He can be as angry as he wants, but hurting the people you love isn't good for anybody," Austin said, "and the only reason for that dog—whether Cowboy or another dog—to be out here and not coming to you is because somebody had it tethered, was training it, or otherwise was doing something to stop him."

"I know," she agreed, "but what I don't know is whether it was really Cowboy or not. As I already told you, it was quite a distance, and just my instincts had me checking it out."

Austin studied her carefully. "I presume those instincts also stopped you from going after it."

She winced and then nodded. "I just had such a horrible

sense of wrongness about the whole thing," she whispered, "and ever since then I've just felt terrible. I'm afraid that Cowboy needed me, and I wasn't there for him. Jesus," she muttered, frustrated at the tears coming, as she brushed them away impatiently. "My father gets angry when my *tender heart gets away from me*," she shared in a mocking tone.

"Don't let him get to you. I understand why he's like that, but it doesn't change the fact that everybody here needs you to have that heart because, without it, what do we have?"

She smiled. "I get what you're saying, but I think you've forgotten how harsh my father can be."

"I haven't forgotten. I just think other things in life are more important than always having to live up to *Daddy's image* of who you are, or should be."

She shook her head. "Believe me, after you left, I didn't have any image to live up to. Dad was devastated."

Austin didn't say anything for a while, then nodded. "Your dad and I were pretty close."

"Yeah, you were, and I wondered sometimes if that wasn't part of the problem."

He frowned at her in astonishment. "What are you talking about?"

She shrugged. "I've always wondered if I'm not any better than Chris because sometimes, you know, I was even jealous of your relationship with Dad."

"Are you kidding? In that man's eyes, the sun itself rises and sets only on you," he declared, staring at her in shock. "How could you possibly think it could be any different?"

"Because, at the end of the day, he always wanted a son," she snapped, shaking her head. "I guess I was just very insecure and needing reassurance, and I couldn't get it," she admitted. "And now that's just one more thing that makes me feel foolish."

"It doesn't matter how it makes you feel now," he pointed out, "but it is something you need to deal with before it destroys something in your life that's special."

She wanted to say it already had, but his gaze had suddenly narrowed to something ahead.

Austin asked her, "How did the War Dog normally react to being out here? Was he comfortable?"

"Cowboy loved it out here and was great with the other animals. He wasn't a cow dog, of course, and didn't have any intention of chasing cattle, but he was always happy to go for a run, always very engaged, very protective," she shared, sounding a bit nostalgic. "God, I really miss him."

"I'm not sure that missing him is exactly what we're looking for right now, but it's obvious that something here still doesn't make any sense." He turned to her. "Are you guys missing any cattle?"

She shook her head. "I can't say that we don't miss a few from time to time, but not to rustlers." He just nodded and didn't say anything. "Chris wouldn't do that anyway," she added, "and no way he would get away with it."

"I would hope not," Austin replied, "but that doesn't mean that whoever is influencing him wouldn't have those skills and the ability to get away with it."

She took a deep breath, then nodded slowly. "That could very well be."

"On the other hand, we don't know that right now, and, until we do, let's just keep it as a possibility to consider—but not the only possibility."

She smiled and nodded. "Yeah, that would be good because I really need it to be anybody but him."

AUSTIN AND ROX returned to the house in silence, and he had a lot to contemplate. Nothing was adding up, but then it never did until you got answers. As he found out in the military, sometimes the answers came, and sometimes they didn't.

Sometimes you had to accept on pure faith that you would never get there, and, as hard as that was, it did happen. But something was going on here that went deeper than that … and was uglier. They didn't see anything suspicious at they went over Cowboy's last day on the ranch with Rox. That didn't sit right with Austin though. He would go back later on his own to see if he could find out what was going on, to see if he found anything in terms of a trail. It had already been weeks, so it's not as if there would be anything obvious. Therefore, he would be looking for what was hard to find.

He planned to go back out tonight and just needed to get permission to take a horse. If not, he would take a ride up the road and maybe park his truck off to the side and walk in the pastures. He just needed to ensure he didn't get shot in the process. Jake was handy with his gun, and, when he was pissed off and upset, he wasn't slow on pulling the trigger, with good reason. When it came to protecting animals on the ranch, you had to have that instinct.

Back at the house, dinner was quiet, as everybody was fairly subdued. The conversation was friendly and polite but fairly nondescript. There was a lot of eyeing around, hoping somebody else would break the silence, and, when nobody did, it basically went back to just a quiet dinner.

Austin's phone buzzed as soon as the meal was over.

He got up, quickly took his plate to the kitchen, then pulled out his phone to check the text, stopping in his tracks to stare at it.

"Something wrong?" Jake asked.

"I'm not sure. I'll let you know in a bit. I'm heading out to meet somebody." And, with that, not letting them know who he just got a text from or where he was going, he walked out to his truck. He could see both Jake and Rox standing out on the front step, watching him. He hopped into his truck, backed around, then headed down the long driveway to the main road. He took a left, going in the opposite direction of town.

He knew they would see his taillights and would start discussing what he was doing, wondering where he was going and why. He didn't necessarily feel the need to fill them in at this point in time. Honestly, he was still trying to figure out what Chris wanted and why he had texted.

As he drove down the road, he pulled onto a side street and then headed down to a small pub that was open late. At least he thought it was still open late. It always had been before. It was also one of the places he used to visit with Chris once in a while, when he just needed to get away. He pulled up and walked into the pub, only to see several men glaring at him, with no friendly faces to be seen.

"We don't like strangers around here," one of the men called out.

"Guess it's a good thing I'm not a stranger," Austin replied, with a wave of his hand.

He walked up to the bar and was relieved when he saw somebody he did know.

The bartender took one look at him and raised his eyebrows. "Good God," he said, as he came around and gave him a big hug. "What the hell, man? We haven't seen you in about five years," he muttered, still shaking his hand. "Not since you got rid of that wife of yours."

"More or less," he replied, with half a nod. "I can't say it was exactly the way I thought my life would go."

"It never is when women are involved," the bartender stated.

Austin chuckled, as he remembered the usual anti-women connotation and banter here. "Apparently the change was good for us."

"Oh, don't tell me that you're back with her."

"No, God no," Austin said, "but we can at least be in the same room and be friendly."

"That's a step forward," he noted, then frowned. "Maybe, but you know what happens when you give them too much leeway."

Austin just nodded and smiled. "Chris been in?" he asked, as he looked around.

"No, not yet, he usually comes in around this time. Have you seen him yet?"

"No, but he texted me to meet him here. Seems like old times."

"Wouldn't it though," the bartended agreed, with a nod. "You guys used to be pretty close."

"We were close. He was on the outs with his family so much, and this was just a place for us to chill and to have a beer without having all that over us."

"Yeah, that poor kid."

"Is he still a poor kid though?" he asked curiously. "It's been five years."

"You wouldn't know it in his case. It feels as if something got stunted along the way," the bartender suggested.

"In a bad way?"

The bartender just looked at him, didn't say anything, and gave an ever-so-slight shrug that didn't mean anything good.

When the door opened, and Chris walked in with a couple buddies, Austin didn't like the look of his friends. Something was wrong with their vibe. There was that slouch of arrogance to them, just something that shouted how they had a hate on for the world, and it looked as if Chris felt he belonged with them.

Chris walked up, saw him, and, instead of giving him a hug or any other friendly greeting, just nodded. "We can talk over here," he said, as he pointed off to the side.

Austin followed him, and his buddies tagged along. He held out his hand and said, "I'm Austin."

The men just looked at his hand, snorted, and walked ahead of him. Austin frowned over at Chris.

Chris just shrugged and explained, "They don't really like strangers."

"Interesting," Austin murmured and followed him to the table at the far end.

He wasn't sure what the hell was going on here, but Austin already recognized the one guy ahead of him, the one with the stubby nose, was the one who had been driving the souped-up truck, while joy-riding on Jake's property. Chris had been in the vehicle too, but Austin wasn't sure about the third one, the skinny younger guy. Austin studied them both, knowing he would try and take photos before he left, but he had to do it without them knowing. He needed to get a little more information on what was going on here.

It was hardly about Cowboy at this point, yet it still could be, in a way. As he sat down, he lifted a hand and ordered himself a beer, politely asking the others if they wanted one. They all just nodded, and, when four beers arrived at the table, he picked his up and took a healthy slug. Then he looked over at Chris. "So, what's going on?"

Chris hesitated, then looked at his buddies, before asking Austin, "What the hell are you doing back?"

"I came in for a job," he replied, with a small smile. "You just never really know when you'll end up in a position of needing to do something, so never say never."

"You shouldn't have come back," Chris replied, "and this is about the only warning I can give you to ensure you get out and stay out."

Austin frowned and asked, "Yeah, and why is that?"

Stubby spoke up. "Because that shit's not happening here anymore. We're not into the old boys' club," he spat in a sour tone, "and we don't like strangers."

"I'm not a stranger," Austin repeated, "so I don't qualify."

"Anybody who hasn't been here in five years is a stranger, and, if you were smart enough to leave in the first place, you should have been smart enough to stay away."

Austin eyed Stubby carefully, trying to figure out what the hell was going on. As far as a shakedown went, this one was lame, and it didn't make a whole lot of sense to him. "What have you got against my being here?" he asked curiously. "I told you. I'm here for work, so what difference does that make to you?"

"If you stick around, you may not like your reception," he added, with a smirk.

"Now why is that?" Austin asked.

Stubby glared at him and said, "Stop talking. We don't fucking like talkers."

"Really?" Austin replied in a calm tone. "Can't say that I ever encountered this attitude when I was here before."

"That's the thing. Times have changed," he stated, "and you aren't welcome."

"I've heard that a time or two in my life," he noted, looking at him, "but it was usually from people I knew, not from complete strangers trying to act tough."

At that, Stubby stiffened and glared at him, and then silence fell over the small room. Harry, the bartender, came over immediately and waved at him. "Hey, Austin."

Austin glanced his way and could see the concern in his eyes. Austin smiled at him. "It's all good. I'm just here saying hi to Chris. After all, no matter where we are now, ... he is still my brother-in-law."

Chris stiffened at that, and the other men turned to glare at Chris.

"What the fuck?" Stubby asked.

Chris shook his head. "He is not exactly that. They've been separated for so damn long, it's not like he's family or anything."

"We're not divorced, so you *are* family," Austin declared, looking at Chris with a hard glance. "Whether you like it or not, or want to admit it or not, ... we *are* family."

Stubby got up and walked out. The other man, Skinny, stared from Chris to Austin and to his buddy who just left. Then Skinny got up and followed suit.

"No family allowed, *huh?*" Austin asked, turning to look at Chris. "Interesting friends you've got there."

Chris flushed and glared at him. "I don't want you ruining things here, man."

"I wasn't aware I was ruining anything," he noted. "I'm not sure what there is to ruin. I know that was you out on the land last night. I'm not sure what the hell you think joy-riding out there will do for you. So, you bust a few fences, let a few cattle loose, pretty petty stuff, so what the hell?"

Chris glared at him. "You don't know anything."

"No, I sure don't, but you should remember one thing about me, Chris. I really don't like having shit go on around me that I don't understand."

Chris shook his head. "Look. You don't want to get involved. I'm not really even a part of this," he added, "but you need to watch your back."

"You know, when you say it like that, … it sounds like a threat."

"No, it's not a threat," he countered, trying for some bravado.

"Is this against your father, your sister, your mother, or what? Because you know that'll never wash with me."

At that he glared at him and added, "You don't know anything."

"No, I don't know. You're right about that. I just came back into town yesterday. All of a sudden, there's a ruckus on the ranch, and I see you out joy-riding. Next thing I know, I'm hearing all kinds of threats, not to mention what you tried to pull here with this shit about *I better get out of town.*" Austin shook his head. "What the hell? Since when is this place so completely anti-people?"

"Since I don't have anything to do with them," he smirked, glaring at him. He tossed back the rest of his beer and added, "If you're smart, you won't either."

"I've never been *not* smart," Austin clarified. "As I told you, … I'm here for a job, and I intend to complete it."

"Yeah, well, I don't give a shit what the job is," Chris said. "So you better get the hell out of town, and this is the only warning you'll get." As he stood up to leave, he caught sight of Austin's pant legs, and the shiny prosthetic sticking out of one.

Austin smiled at Chris's reaction. "One of the things I'm here for is to retrieve a stolen War Dog. The War Department sent me to find him."

At that, Chris stiffened and muttered, "What the hell are you talking about?"

"I think you know," Austin said, "but it sure as hell better not be anything to do with me and the job that I'm here for because that's an entirely different story."

"What? Hang on a minute. … You're here for a fucking dog?"

"I'm here for a fucking *War Dog*," Austin confirmed, with a nod, "and, if I need to be here for other shit while I'm at it, you can bet I'll be right in the middle of it."

Chris shook his head. "Man, have you ever screwed yourself up. … I don't know what the hell you're still sniffing around my sister for because she made it pretty damn clear you weren't wanted here."

"She absolutely did," he agreed. "And you're right. I would be pretty foolish to go back down that pathway again. But it's got nothing to do with you whether I do or I don't. It's my business, and no one has a say in it, including you. Besides, I'm here for something completely unrelated and didn't come here to see your sister at all, but again that is my business."

"*Right*," Chris replied in a jeering tone.

"But what I'm seeing is somebody with a big-man act, something stuck up his ass, causing problems that he seems to think some criminal activity will make better."

"Nothing criminal about it," Chris spat. "This is all about getting even."

And, with that, Chris stormed out the door of the pub.

CHAPTER 6

R OX WOKE UP the next morning, wondering if she'd gotten any sleep in between all the times she had woken up. After Austin had left last night, she and her dad had talked some about where he might be going and what he might be up to, but neither of them had any freaking idea. Austin had come home and had gone straight to bed, without saying anything to anybody.

She was fully prepared to brace him about it this morning. As she got down early enough to set up coffee and to arrive first, she found him sitting in the kitchen, talking to her father, and obviously the conversation wasn't going well. She stepped in and glared at Austin. "You sure know how to cause trouble when you get home."

Jake sucked in his breath. "That ain't fair," he snapped. "You don't even know what the hell's going on."

"Maybe not"—she glared back at her dad—"but it's obvious that you're upset."

Jake's gaze softened, and he shrugged. "Sure, I'm pissed off, and I'm upset, but I'm not upset at Austin. There's a big difference. You need to know the truth and to direct your anger where it belongs."

As it was a rebuke that was probably well deserved, she flushed and tried to hide it, then walked over to the kitchen area to put on coffee, only to find a fresh pot already sitting there. She poured herself a cup and headed back to the men. "In that case, maybe you should tell me exactly what's going on."

"I met with Chris last night," Austin shared.

"Chris?" She stared at him. "He texted you?"

Austin nodded. "Yeah, he sent me a text to meet him down at Rusty's Pub."

She shook her head. "Why the hell it's called Rusty's Pub when it's Harry's, … I don't know."

"I don't know either," Austin noted, "but it doesn't matter because some things never change. Harry is still a wife-hater, and the pub is still for his select few clientele."

"I think they keep that place going just fine," she muttered, staring at him, "and, honest to God, they're all misfits in there anyway."

"Maybe, but that's where Chris was. And several of his cronies."

"Of course he was." She groaned, then frowned at Austin, curiosity in her eyes. "What did he have to say?"

"I'm not sure what's going on, but he told me how this is all about revenge and didn't have a whole lot else to say."

"Revenge for what?" she asked, staring at him.

"I don't know, but he's hanging out with two strange characters, both very unfriendly, and when they found out I was still family, one got up and walked out, clearly quite pissed off. Apparently Chris hadn't told him."

Rox frowned. "Interesting. … I guess technically you are still family."

"Yeah, technically I am," he confirmed casually, "so it wasn't a lie. Of course that set them off because Chris hadn't told them about the relationship,"

"What did they want though?" she asked.

"I'm not sure about what they want, but Chris wanted to send me a not-so-friendly warning to get the hell out of town."

At that, Jake and Rox both stared at him dumbly. "Seriously?" Jake asked, still looking at him but not seeing him.

Austin nodded. "Yes, seriously, and I'm not sure what they're planning, but Chris has got some kind of hate going for this family."

"Yeah, I'm not surprised," she muttered, "but I didn't think it extended to me."

"I'm not sure it does. Yet, if push comes to shove, will it or won't it? I don't know. What I can tell you is that I wouldn't trust him or any of his so-called friends right now."

She slumped in her chair. "I don't know when the hell everything blew up, but, man, Chris is not the forgiving kind."

"No, and in a way he's very much like your old man here," Austin pointed out, with a nod toward the man sitting silently in front of him.

Jake snorted. "You're the only one who ever talks to me like that."

"That's because I spent a lot of time in the military," Austin explained. "I've been yelled at by the best of them, and I'm not afraid of you, never have been."

"Christ, I don't want anybody afraid of me," Jake muttered, reaching up a huge, calloused hand and rubbing his face.

Austin smiled at the older man. "You're looking for what you used to have," he offered in a quiet voice. "Ranch hands you can count on, as in the olden days. When they stayed at the ranch, when they worked for decades, sometimes retiring here on the property and embracing the life that went along with that," Austin described, "but times have changed. It doesn't mean that they're any better or worse, but they're definitely different."

Jake looked at him reluctantly and nodded. "We also don't have the money we used to earn from ranching," he shared, "and it's really burning my boat to think we might lose it all."

"Are you close to losing it all?" Austin asked in surprise. "You guys were doing very well when I left."

"We were, but then you left," Jake stated, cracking a smile, "and, no, not because you left. You were in the military even then."

Austin nodded. "I was and still would be, if I hadn't gotten hurt."

"Something you don't talk about," she pointed out.

"Nothing to talk about. I was injured in the line of work, and I could have taken a desk job with the navy if I wanted to, but that wasn't what I wanted to do," he shared.

Jake nodded. "It would kill me."

Austin laughed. "You think anything that stops you from riding a horse for sixteen hours a day would kill you."

Jake grinned. "You're not wrong," he muttered, "not wrong at all."

"So, why does Chris feel the need for revenge?" Austin asked.

"I don't know, unless it's literally got to do with not getting the ranch."

"Why would he think he should get it anyway? That's the part I don't understand. If he's never had that expectation, why would he be disappointed to hear it would be otherwise? And ..." Austin turned to Rox. "I don't remember there ever being any discord between the two of you."

She shook her head. "I would have said there wasn't, until the last few years. However, if he's doing this to hurt the ranch, … then, of course, he's also doing it to hurt me."

Austin thought about it and then nodded. "It's definitely targeted. What do you know about these other two guys he hangs around with?" He described Stubby and Skinny to Rox and Jake.

"Outside of being just straight-up trouble," Jake replied, "I don't know anything. One of them comes from a pretty wealthy family in town. His father passed away recently, and the uncle has just taken over."

"So, maybe a case of sour grapes all around? Maybe that one expected to get his father's ranch too?" Austin guessed.

Jake looked at him and then slowly nodded. "That could be it. Maybe they're just triggering each other," he suggested, then shook his head. "But what the hell? Since when is that a thing? What's wrong with the younger generation today?"

Austin smiled at him. "The same thing that was wrong with them a long time ago," he said, with a smirk. "It's not that people have changed that much, but circumstances and times have changed, and there's always that expectation of … entitlement."

"That's the thing that really gets me, … that entitlement." Jake snorted. "This place is all I have, and it's been in my family since … forever. Chris is a part of my family, and I certainly did not cut him out," he stated. "You've got to understand that. It's not that Chris wouldn't get anything, and nobody would get all of it at any time. He would be a contributing partner and a part owner, living and working here," he explained. "He just didn't like the numbers."

"And the numbers were?"

Jake looked over at Rox, then back at Austin, and reluctantly replied, "Seventy-five and twenty-five."

He nodded. "So, 25 percent wasn't enough for him?"

"I'm not sure anything would have been enough for him," Rox interjected, "and I guess it probably would burn Chris to think that he wouldn't even get half, but it's also not something he wants to work at. This isn't where he wants to be, and I don't think he really wants anything to do with the land."

"Did you consider, instead of offering that, potentially giving him a cash settlement instead?" Austin asked.

Jake shook his head. "We're a little on the cash-shy side of the things right now," he pointed out, "and I didn't feel as if I owed him anything. I married his mama, and I raised him. There was never any child support contributions made from that sorry, no-good father of his, and raising even one child isn't cheap. Chris was taught the value of a good day's work. He was offered the opportunity to go on for more education and declined, and he still would never come and help us work the ranch. So, I don't know what the hell he expected."

"He expected a handout apparently," Austin replied. "I'm wondering why it came to this. Is there anybody else in his life who would have had that kind of influence on him?"

"Just his mother," Jake noted, "and you know how Amie feels about handouts."

Austin almost laughed at that because Amie was a hell of a worker herself, always had been, always would be. She didn't have any thought that the world owed her or anyone else a living, yet apparently, somewhere along the line, Chris had adopted this mind-set. At some point in time Chris had decided that Jake owed him a living.

"I wonder how much of this is hurt, how much of this is

that sense of entitlement, and how much of it is just anger in the moment. Maybe it's all of that pushed into something that he's not sure how to get out of right now, or even knows that he should get out of," Austin murmured, thinking out loud.

Rox looked at him. "Sounds as if you do remember what Chris was like."

"Sure, I do," he stated, "and I also remembered as soon as I saw him last night that he was always heavily influenced by those around him, and that is unfortunate. He's older than you by what?" He frowned as he thought about it. "Four, five years?"

"Five." She nodded. "Yet, if he's dealing with people like those at Rusty's Pub, where women are seen as next to nothing and shouldn't even be allowed to own property, ... I can only imagine how that may have screwed with his head."

"Got to love that sexist attitude still hanging on out there," Austin muttered, with a headshake, "and you're right. It'll just keep firing up that resentment. One, you're female, and two, he's the elder son."

Rox grimaced. "Yeah, it's got to be something like that."

"What about his dad?" Austin asked.

"No idea, I've never really met him."

He looked at her in surprise. "All this time living with Chris, and you haven't met his dad?"

"Not really. Seen him at a distance once or twice, picking up or dropping off Chris. Remember that Chris lived with his father for a time, but it didn't seem like that extended visitation went that well. Chris came back with a bad attitude, and, as far as I know, he's not in contact with his father now."

"Yet it's quite possible that he's getting fed something

dysfunctional along that line from somebody, so we have to take a closer look at who those somebodies are."

She snorted. "Anybody in town who's feeling as if they're hard done by," she suggested, "that's who."

"Maybe, and it could just be this group of friends I just met, especially if—what was his name? Todd? If this guy Todd was cut out of his inheritance or just feels like it because his uncle is now running the family business, then it really could be just angry men sitting around with no jobs, keeping each other stirred up. I hate to say it, but they can be quite dangerous."

"Yeah, so we've noticed," Rox noted sarcastically.

Austin turned to her. "You know, Rox. You can cut out the attitude at any time. I came here to solve the War Dog problem, and I can just do that and leave, or I can stand by and try to help out," he clarified, and enough hardness filled his tone for her to shift back. "But, either way, I'm really not into facing arguments and bad attitudes all the time." And, with that, Austin got up, refilled his coffee, and sat back down again.

Jake looked at him, over at his daughter, then shrugged and interjected, "You guys need to work this out. We tried so hard back then, and it didn't do a damn bit of good. You still left."

"I left because I was given an ultimatum," Austin reminded them both, "and I didn't like it."

"You didn't take the ultimatum very well." Jake nodded glumly.

"We all suffered for that too," Austin declared, "but, right now, that is not the foremost problem in my world."

Jake said, "You guys will either make it or you won't. Then you'll get divorced, and maybe she'll move on. I don't know, and I don't care. We invested heavily the first time around, but I don't think we'll do it again."

She stared at her father, and Austin could see the hurt in her eyes. Yet he understood. They'd all been really close and the separation, as it had happened, had hurt a lot of people. At the same time, Austin also understood that Rox had probably paid a much higher price than she had ever intended.

He turned his attention back to the problem at hand. "Does Chris have access to everything on the ranch?"

Jake growled at him. "As in what? We've got cattle out there in open pastures."

"Is he an animal lover or an animal hater?"

"Neither. I think he considered the animals a paycheck," Jake replied. "Other than that, … he didn't really have a whole lot to do with them."

"You're not having any rustling issues, so what problem could Chris possibly have, and does he have any legal leg to stand on?"

"Legal?" Jake eyed him in surprise. "I don't think he's got any legal standing at all. Why would you say that?"

"Because the other guy—Stubby, aka Todd—appeared to be the leader, and I had my boss look him up. He's the son of a lawyer, … and he's actually quietly doing his own legal work."

"Legal work?" Jake repeated. "One of the group with Chris?"

Austin nodded. "The one who left first, Todd, as soon as he found out Chris and I were still family."

At that, Jake sat back, clearly confused. "It's not as if I have anything that Chris could challenge in some way," he muttered. "Yes, there's a will, but it's filed with the lawyer—

a good lawyer at that. He passed away not very long ago, and that was upsetting, but … age will do that."

"What happened to the will then?" Austin asked.

"What do you mean?" Jake asked.

"Who is looking after your legal matters now?"

"Another law firm in town. Why?"

"Because I'm a little worried that there might be some legal finagling going on. I just need to know that you have that will locked down, safe and secure, that it still says what you want it to say."

At that, Jake hopped to his feet, gave him a hard look, then took off to his home office.

Rox looked over at Austin, frowning. "They can't really do anything about that, can they?"

"It depends on whether they're planning on killing your father or not," Austin shared in a low tone, "and believe me that your father got that message pretty-damn fast."

"Jesus," she muttered, "I don't want that to happen."

"None of us do," Austin said. "I don't know to what extent any of this can be done legally or with so much finagling that it'll be tied up in the courts for a long time. Meanwhile, they could be up to something. It all sounds far-fetched, I know, but it depends on how much Chris really thinks he's owed this ranch."

"He's not owed anything," she stated, staring at him. "I'm not owed anything. It's my father's family's inheritance, and his legacy to do with as he chooses. None of us are owed any part of it."

"I understand, and that's part of the problem. Maybe Chris somehow had this expectation all along. I just don't know where he would have got it from."

At that, a tired and worn-out voice came from the doorway. "From me probably."

He turned to see Amie, standing in the doorway. She used to get massive migraines, and it looked as if she had one coming on right now. He helped her to a chair and asked, "And why is that?"

"Because he always wanted to play farmer, and he always wanted to play rancher, and we used to joke about it all being his someday," Amie explained, "but he was just a little child at the time. Rox hadn't even been born, and Jake's grandfather was still alive."

"So, maybe, somewhere along the line in those early years, he got this idea in his head that someday it would all be his?" Austin asked.

"But it was just a game we played," she whispered, "and it would never have involved hurting anybody."

"Unless he believed he wasn't getting what he thought he deserved."

"Depends on who he is influenced by at the moment. I don't like anything about this conversation," she whispered, wiping a hand across her forehead. "It never occurred to me that my son would feel this way about his stepdad, who took him in and who did so much for him."

"But, in Chris's mind, you also had another child, and he lost out because of it."

Amie snorted at that. "Welcome to life. We've all lost out on various things we would have liked to have had go differently. That's just life."

"Would Chris's father have reinforced that *he's lost out* feeling?"

She nodded slowly. "Yes, Chris's biological father was very much a person who believed the world owed him everything," she murmured. She looked back over at Rox.

"Remember when Chris came back from his father's that one time? All Chris could talk about was how his dad would buy him a new motorbike, so he would have the best motorbike on the place?"

Rox frowned at that, as if trying to search out the memory, then her face cleared as she remembered. "I do remember that, and then the bike never showed up, and Chris was devastated."

"Exactly. And that was his father, through and through. He used to make big promises and then never follow through with any of them."

"What ended up happening?" Austin asked.

"Honestly, Jake bought him one, a really nice one. No, not better than everybody else's, but something that would work nicely for here, for this land and for this space," she clarified. "I just don't think Chris ever really understood that he wouldn't get everything he was always expecting and demanding. I mean, none of us do. Yet Chris saw it as a consolation prize for having lost his father and for being second best to Rox somehow."

"He wasn't ever second best though," Rox stated painfully. "Is all this about me? Is he focused on hurting me because of all this?"

"Quite possibly, yes," Austin stated, looking at her. "If you're the one who's inheriting the bulk of it, then it's quite possible that's what it's all about."

"That's ridiculous," Amie wailed, as she continued to massage her temples. "It doesn't make any sense."

"And yet, in his childish mind, he might have very well been thinking that he is now family and that he does deserve to have a full share, at least equal to Rox's."

"But he's demanding it all, which is total nonsense. And

after all this, … no way he'll be getting anything because of the way he's acting," Amie said, staring at him, "so that makes even less sense."

"Depends on if … depends on what their plans are. … I know it's far-fetched, and I don't even want to bring it up because we haven't gotten very far down this pathway. Also we don't know just how dedicated Chris and his buddies are. But, considering whatever trouble is happening, what if neither Rox nor Jake were still around to inherit anything?"

Amie frowned. "Everything goes to me, and I don't know whether the will's been changed or not, but it still won't go to Chris."

"And if something happens to you?" Austin asked.

She paled, pinched her lips together, and whispered, "I have a will myself, and mine says that everything I have … goes to my husband first, then to Rox second," Amie shared. "Except for a few things in a trust fund that I set up for Chris, he gets nothing else."

"Did you ever turn over his trust to him?" Austin asked.

"No," Amie said, shaking her head. "It was supposed to take effect when he turns thirty-five, but I changed the age because it seems as if he's always been on the brink of problems."

"Are you sure you didn't tell him at some point about this trust?"

"I might have." She shrugged. "At one point I realized that he should be mature enough to handle it, and I was really afraid of the outcome."

"Even though you say he doesn't know about it, I'm not sure we can trust that. Over all these years, it would have been so easy to say something, like, *Oh, honey, it'll be okay. You'll be taken care of, not to worry.*"

She flushed at that and then nodded. "I can see myself telling him something like that, particularly when he was being difficult, but I certainly wouldn't have taken anything away from Rox."

"No, but she was already well covered with the larger share and the controlling interest in the ranch, per Jake's will, so, unless Chris got everything else, it would appear to him as if he wasn't getting his full share again. When did you change the age on the trust fund?"

She frowned and sighed. "Gosh, I don't know. It was after you left. Soon after one of the times Chris and Jake got so riled about everything," she shared.

"So, in the last few years?"

"No, wait," she corrected, "not that long ago. It was this last year."

"You mean, when all this trouble started on the ranch?"

She frowned and then slowly and reluctantly nodded. "That's possible, yes."

Austin continued. "So, we have an angry son, who's only getting a minor share of the ranch from his stepdad, was expecting to get a trust fund that you had set up from your own inheritance, I presume?"

She nodded. "From my family, yes."

"Money that you surely could have used when you were a single parent, but you set aside for him?"

She nodded again.

"So, now he finds out that you've changed the age on his trust, and he has to wait how many more years?"

"I changed it to forty," she replied. "So, in theory, he still has to go another ten years from now."

"So, you did it just before he was about to turn thirty?" he asked, feeling his own incredulity kicking in.

She winced and nodded. "Yes."

"So had you changed it before?"

She nodded, rubbing her face. "Yes, I kept thinking he would grow up."

"So, each time he got closer to getting that trust, you've changed the age."

She stared at him, tears coming to her eyes, as she slowly nodded. "Oh my God, I did this, didn't I?"

"It doesn't matter who did what at this point. The problem though is that, in Chris's mind, he's probably now taking it all to mean that he'll never get anything. While we don't know for sure how he handled it or what he actually knows, but, if you dangled that carrot once or twice and then pulled it away from him, that combined with finding out he's not the heir apparent to Jake's ranch, we have a very angry man who had expectations that have now been taken from him."

Amie slumped deeper into her chair, pinching the bridge of her nose. "I did it because he was being so irrational," she explained. "I didn't want him to just take that money and to blow through it. It's not a lot of money, but it's enough that would have set him up nicely, if only he would be responsible with it."

"That's the thing about trust funds though," Austin noted. "You hand them out, but you don't get to dictate what people do with it."

She bit her lip and nodded. "The lawyer did say something like that to me, but he also told me it was my money, and I can do what I wanted with it," she told them. "I didn't want my son to just blow it all. His friends are rough. I thought that he was using drugs, and I just didn't want it to go by the wayside."

Austin nodded in understanding. "Oh, I get it. I totally understand, but I highly doubt that Chris did."

"No, he didn't." She nodded. "He was pretty angry when he came to me, asking how much money was in his trust and when he would get it. That was when he was turning twenty-five, and I told him that I'd raised it to thirty, and he was beyond angry," she explained. "Then, when he got close to thirty, I realized he wouldn't change, so I raised it again, and yes," she admitted, "if I need to, I will raise it again."

"I'm surprised the lawyers have it set up that way," Austin noted.

"It's a different kind of a trust," she said, "and I don't even know if *trust* is the right word for it, but he was supposed to get this chunk of money when I deemed him suitable."

"And you haven't deemed him suitable?"

"No," she stated defiantly. "He's just been hell on wheels, and getting that money would not benefit him at all."

Austin didn't say anything for a moment and just sat back and nodded. "I don't have any kids, so I can't imagine. But one of the things I do know is that the minute you try to dictate what they do with anything, it's enough to mess things up on a pretty big scale," he shared.

"Which apparently is what you think I've done," Amie said, staring at him. The tears were still in her eyes, but so was that hard glare of a woman who had been through tough times and had come out the other side and wasn't prepared to give an inch.

He smiled at her and replied, "It's your money, and, in retrospect, it would have been better to *not* tell him about it, and he could have gotten it if and when you ever felt he was ready to have it. If you didn't want to give it to him, it would come to him at your deathbed, if that's how you wanted to dole it out. This way, it's more like, *if you behave yourself, we'll give it to you. However, if you don't, we're not.* Since Chris was already a pretty angry man, it's likely been just enough to fuel that fire."

"Even if it is him," Rox jumped in, unable to stay silent any longer, "that still doesn't explain what he's doing and what he's planning."

"No, it doesn't, but he is planning something, and it's all about revenge. I thought maybe it was revenge against Jake, but it could very easily be revenge against all of you. You because you exist," he said, pointing to Rox, "and I know that's not fair, but that doesn't really matter when you're as angry as Chris is. Because of what Amie's been doing with this trust money, and Jake because he wants the ranch to stay whole and to remain in his family's bloodline, all just makes Chris angrier and angrier."

Rox groaned. "So, we are all on his hit list."

"We don't know if there even is a hit list. All of this is wrapped up for a fire that anybody close to him could very easily set off. What I don't know is what they have planned. That's what we have to figure out before he gets a chance to put those plans into motion," Austin said, "and I need to find out if it has anything to do with Cowboy."

"What could it possibly have to do with him?" Amie asked, staring at him. "Chris doesn't even like animals."

"I know, but what does Rox really love?"

"Animals," Amie muttered, without even thinking about it.

"So how can Chris hurt Rox the most?" Austin asked.

At that, both of them winced.

Austin nodded. "Now the question is whether he's done something to hurt that animal, in which case that'll set off a whole different level of anger on my side. Or did he just take Cowboy, making sure you suffer"—he pointed to Rox—"and that is something else altogether."

"It doesn't make any sense that he would go to all this trouble," Rox murmured.

"Maybe not, but it could also mean that he was a prime target for somebody else, who might have something else in mind. If Chris has no money, how is he making any? Jake mentioned he was just working part time, but is he working full time now?"

"I don't know," Amie murmured. "That's something we'll need to find out."

He nodded. "In that case I guess that's where I'm going next," Austin announced. "I need to make a few phone calls and also a few visits in town. I'll be gone for a good share of the day, and then I'll head back out and see what I can find out about where Cowboy went."

"You really think you'll find anything?" Rox asked, staring at him. "It's been weeks."

"Yeah, it's been weeks, but that doesn't mean there isn't evidence somewhere along the line," he stated, "and, if it's there, … I'll find it."

Rox knew better than to doubt Austin, and if anything good could come from any of this, it was that he was back, at least for the moment. He had always been the kind of person who, when he said he would do something, he would do it. Whether you liked it or not, he was there, and he would follow through. The trouble was, all too often nobody really liked what he had to do, including him, but he never shirked that duty, and, like her, always stepped up to the plate and did what he needed to do.

Now, for the first time, she wondered at how crazy and lost her life had been since he had walked.

AUSTIN PARKED NEAR the mechanic's garage, hopped out, then checked his gait because his prosthetic was starting to be a bit of a pain again. Kat would say he was just on it too much, and that was probably the truth too. He walked up to the open garage doors to see several mechanics working away under vehicles. A man shouted at him from across the garage, and he headed in that direction. He didn't see any sign of Chris, but that didn't mean anything. A number of people were underneath vehicles, and Austin couldn't even begin to sort out who was here and who wasn't.

As he stepped into the office, he looked over at a man who seemed vaguely familiar. The man frowned at him. "Jesus Christ," he muttered. "Austin, right?"

"Yeah, that's me," he replied, with a smile, "Jenson, is it? It's nice to come back where people know you."

"Depends whether they want to see you again or not," he teased, with half a grin.

"To the best of my knowledge, I didn't leave on bad terms, so it would be a surprise if there were any hard feelings in that direction."

"I thought you and the wife split."

"We did," he agreed, "but life is far too short to hold grudges."

His eyebrows shot up. "That's true, but that's not the way I heard it." Jenson looked around behind Austin.

Austin didn't need to turn around to know who he was referring to, so he shrugged. "Lots of people think they know what's going on, but unless you're one of the two people married to each other," he explained, "you really don't know shit."

"That's the way of it, all right. So, what can I do for you today?" he asked, eyeing him closely.

Austin smiled. "I've got some questions I'm looking to ask. Have you got a place we can talk?"

The boss nodded. "I guess so. Any reason you want it to be private?" Then he led the way to the back room.

"Yeah, there is." When the door closed behind him, he asked, "Have you seen a big dog around here, a big dark Malinois?"

He nodded. "Sure. Over the years there's been a bunch of them. Why?"

"I'm here on behalf of the War Department," he began, handing him a card. "We're looking for one that went missing here a few weeks back."

His eyebrows shot up, and he stared at him. "The War Department," he repeated in disbelief.

"Yes, the missing dog I'm looking for is a K9 War Dog. He did his duty overseas and was released to a family here and has since gone missing. We're trying to locate him."

Jenson shook his head, as he stared at Austin. "Don't that beat all? Who would have thought the government had any money for this shit."

"Doesn't mean they have money or not, but a separate company handles the search and retrieval of these animals."

"Wow," he muttered, as he sat back in his wooden chair. "Well shit, yeah, … I've seen one around, a couple times."

"Yeah? Any idea who with or where?"

"Sure, Chris, right here," he replied. "I've seen him with one."

"Recently?"

"I think so. I'm not sure it was in the last couple weeks, but I know he's been around with a dog."

Austin hadn't thought to ask Rox if Chris would have hidden the dog someplace.

The owner added, "You should be talking to your ex-wife about that."

"I have been," he replied, with a smile. "It makes for interesting conversations."

He started to laugh at that. "Don't that beat all. You leave in a huff, and you come back because of a dog. If it ain't one bitch, it's another."

Knowing that would be a recurring joke around the place, Austin just shook his head and ignored it. "She didn't have anything to do with it," he noted, "and that isn't exactly the way I would want it discussed."

"No, maybe not," he conceded, "but people will be people."

And that was very much the truth. Austin looked around and asked, "Can you remember the last time you saw the dog?"

He sat back, kicked his heels up on the desk, and gave it some thought. "I'm not sure. You would have to talk to Chris about it."

"Yeah, I want to, but, when I found him at the pub last night, his buddies didn't take to me that well."

At that, Jenson's feet slammed to the floor, and he glared. "You watch those ones." He waved a finger in the air. "That is not a group you want to cross."

"Maybe not," Austin said, "but, if they're looking for

trouble, they found it."

His eyebrows shot up, and he nodded. "I remember you were always kind of like that, weren't you? People make comments you don't like, and you get a little testy about it."

"No, not testy," he clarified, "but some of the shit that they were talking about last night didn't make me happy."

"Chris is one angry guy," the owner shared, with a note of warning, "so you'd best stay out of that mess."

Austin shrugged. "Easier said than done."

"No, it's not *easier said than done*, just do it," he snapped, with a headshake. "I don't know what's going on with him and those friends of his, but they're trouble. You need to stay away. Otherwise ..."

"Otherwise, what?" he challenged.

At that, the other man backed down. "I don't know *what*," he admitted, "but it ain't gonna be good."

"Thanks for the warning. I appreciate it. How often does Chris work for you here?"

"It used to be every day," he replied, "but now it's just a few days a week."

"Hard to pay bills on that."

"I know. That's what I told him when he wanted me to cut his hours, but he didn't want to tell me what he would be doing in the meantime. I'm short on good mechanics around this place, and, even though he's not licensed, he's got a knack for it," he muttered. "But I don't know what his deal is, and I don't know what's going on with that group he runs with, but I know it can't be good." He gave another warning. "Honest to God, nobody else does either, and it's probably better if you keep it that way too."

"That bad, *huh?*"

"Yeah, ... that bad," he agreed, with a look out toward

his shop. "I've been here a long time, and you get to know the ones who are trouble."

"Oh, I hear you," Austin confirmed. "It's the same as when you're out fighting any enemy. You know who on your team you can count on, and who are the ones you would just as soon get reassigned."

He snorted. "Been there, done that too. Spent a fair bit of time in the service myself," he shared. "I was happy to take my leave of it, but, while I was there, it wasn't all bad, and it made a man out of me. I needed that at the time, and I sure wish some of these young punks would be forced to do a tour, just to kick some of that nonsense out of their heads."

"Or at least make them work for a living," Austin added.

"Isn't that the truth? Anyway I can't always stop and shoot the breeze, but you're welcome to come back any time," the owner offered, as he hopped to his feet. "In the meantime, I've got work to do. You're not a mechanic by any chance?" he asked hopefully.

"Nope, I'm sure not," Austin said, with a smile, "but I'll keep it in mind, if I see anybody who's looking for work."

"Yeah, you do that. I've got more than I can handle right now, and, with Chris down to just a few days, that isn't helpful."

"Yeah, I hear you," he muttered.

He stepped out to find Chris standing there, glaring at him. "What the hell are you doing back here?" he asked in a rough tone, but his boss hollered at him.

"He's here because I asked him to come in here," he snapped. "Now get your ass back to work."

Chris just glared at the two of them and stomped off.

As Austin turned to head out to his vehicle, Jenson added, "I mean it. Something bad is going on around here. You better stay out of it, if you can."

And, with that, Austin headed outside, but he could tell that he was under watch. As he turned, he saw two men in mechanics' overalls, standing there, staring at him, and had stopped working to do that.

One made a gesture with his finger which Austin knew perfectly well, but it was interesting that he felt the need to. The other one didn't say a word, just stared at him. He might not be as expressive, but there was a threat in his gaze. There was just something very dead looking about those eyes.

Austin hopped back into his truck and headed over to see the lawyer Jake had engaged after the death of his long-time attorney. As he walked in the attorney's office, the receptionist looked at him and frowned, and he frowned right back.

"He's not taking walk-in appointments today."

"Really? And when is he taking appointments?" he asked curiously.

She flushed. "I would have to look at his calendar, but he's a very busy man."

"Right, and I would assume that is the goal," he noted, "but I suggest you let him decide today." She stiffened and glared at him. "Unless we'll have a problem?"

"I don't know what problem you're suggesting," she spat, scrunching up her nose. "He's a very busy man, and he doesn't meet with people just walking in off the street."

He cracked up at that. "Lady, in a town like this, we both know he's more than happy to meet with people dropping in off the street."

"He's just not anybody's lawyer," she stated, with a glare in his direction.

"Oh, well, that's good to know." He stepped outside and phoned Jake, then told him what happened.

"What the hell?" Jake asked.

"Yeah, so I suggest you come in here, find yourself another lawyer, and transfer all your documents somewhere else."

"Good Christ, as if I need this today," he muttered. "Somebody's poisoned one of the wells on the back forty."

"Damn, though I have to say I'm not surprised,. While I have a damn good idea who did it, I'm just not sure I completely understand the why."

"If it's that piece-of-shit stepson of mine," he yelled, "believe me that I'll be pressing charges."

"I know," Austin agreed, "but, before we end up with a completely catastrophic failure of relationships, you need to ensure you've got a rock-solid will in place."

"Jesus Christ." He started to swear again. "I'll be in town in twenty minutes."

As Jake went to ring off, Austin added, "Jake, please drive carefully."

That shut up the old man as nothing else would have, and he hung up very quickly.

With that done, Austin headed back onto the sidewalk, where he stood looking over toward the entrance to the lawyer's office. Sure enough, a lawyer-looking guy raced out of the office, heading for his vehicle.

Austin stepped in his way. "Hey, aren't you John Dikam?" he asked.

The other man frowned and nodded. "Yes, that's me. Why?"

"I was just in there, trying to talk to you, but your secretary is quite the guardian of your time."

"Well, yes, I'm a very busy man." He glared at him. "What do you want?" And his tone was so unfriendly and antagonistic that it set all of Austin's hackles on edge.

"I was looking to find a lawyer, but I guess that's not really possible with your attitude. Guess there are plenty of lawyers in town to choose from."

"Are there?" he asked.

"There was a really good lawyer, somebody we could all count on and could trust, who upheld the law and looked out for his clients," Austin shared, shaking his head, "but I understand that he died. I'm about to head over to the police station to have a look at the autopsy and see if everything is on the up-and-up involving his death."

"What are you talking about?" the attorney asked in bewilderment.

"I just want to confirm that nothing is suspicious about the way he died."

Dikam's face turned a molten color. "What the hell?" he sputtered. "Did you just accuse me of murder?"

"No," he replied, keeping his tone simple and casual. "I don't even know you, do I? Hell, I can't even get an appointment to come in and talk to you."

"And I wouldn't talk to you now either," he declared, "not with that attitude."

As the man raced over to his vehicle, Austin called out behind him, "That's too bad, since I know somebody who's on his way in to talk to you."

He froze and asked, "Who?"

"One of your clients, who needed a helping hand today. I was supposed to come in and talk to you about it, but apparently, unless I'm previously vetted, I don't even get into your office."

The irritated man stopped and glared at him. "I don't know what game you're playing, young man, but I don't fool around. My clients are very important."

Austin had to laugh at that because this guy was maybe forty years old, but he wouldn't even count on that. "Yeah? Unless they're clients you're avoiding."

"What are you talking about?" Dikam asked in exasperation. "I'm not avoiding anybody."

"*Right*," Austin said, with a smirk. "So why don't you hang around until your client arrives?"

"Because I have another appointment."

"Yeah, where?" he asked, genuinely curious.

"None of your business," Dikam snapped, as he loosened the collar around his neck.

"I see you've got Chris Remington as a client," he noted.

Dikam's eyes widened. "I don't talk to anybody about my clients. There is such a thing as confidentiality."

Austin nodded. "There are also things such as illegal proceedings, particularly when conducted by a lawyer."

Dikam froze and some of the color drained from his face, as Austin just watched with interest. It had been a shot in the dark and something to rattle Dikam. Apparently it had hit home.

Dikam looked terrified, and, with that, Austin knew, without a doubt, that he was on the right track. "Still don't want to wait for your client?"

Dikam stood here, rooted to the spot for a moment, and then shrugged. "You haven't even told me who it is," he stated, "and all I'm hearing from you are innuendos and threats, and I don't appreciate it."

"Threats? Is that what you're hearing? Because honest to God, I didn't threaten you at all. I just wanted to get in to see you, or at least get an appointment, but apparently you've got your dragon of a secretary not letting anybody in."

"You definitely need an appointment," he declared. "That's how I prefer to handle my business."

"Ah, that's how handle your business, *huh*?" Austin nodded. "As I remember, Richards was very open and friendly with his clients."

"As you apparently already know, he's dead."

"I know, that's why I'm heading over to the sheriff's department to check if it was a suspicious death."

"Of course it wasn't," Dikam stated in exasperation. "The man had a heart attack."

"*Hmm*, that's interesting. A heart attack, *huh*? I wonder if it was induced by somebody's extra efforts? I'll have to look into that too." And, with that, he slowly turned and sauntered back to his truck.

"Wait, wait, wait. What are you talking about? Why are you even thinking that? What is going on here?"

Clearly rattled, Dikam called out after Austin, seemingly trying to sort out what was going on and who the hell he even was because, so far, nobody had even asked Austin for his name, something he found fascinating.

"Oh, I don't think it matters to you much," Austin noted and kept on walking.

Just then, a vehicle came ripping in around the corner, screeching to a stop next to Austin's truck.

Dikam looked over at Austin and frowned. "See? That's what I mean. Everybody in far too big of a hurry in this town."

"Richards didn't die suddenly though," Austin stated.

"What are you talking about?" Dikam asked, shaking his

head in disgust. "I don't understand why you're here hassling me, but I'm just about done with it."

"Yeah? You might be just about done with it, or maybe, just maybe, you're about to be right in the middle of it."

At that moment, Jake walked into view and glared at Dikam. "I need to talk to you," he snapped and motioned him to the door of his office.

Dikam seemed to shrink, but then that was Jake. He was huge, rough, and had a heart of gold, yet nobody would dare to cross him.

"He wouldn't even let me in his personal office," Austin shared cheerfully, knowing things were about to get very interesting, "and I am not even sure he knows who you are."

"He damn well better know who I am," Jake snapped, glaring at Dikam. "Don't you?" The lawyer opened his mouth, but Jake railroaded right over him. "I've just talked to Teglish around the corner," he shared, "and I'm transferring all my legal documentation over to him."

Dikam started to sputter. "What? Why are you doing that?" he asked, red in the face. "I've been nothing but amiable and helpful."

"*Sure*, you have," Jake snorted. "Until all that shit that my son started, you were fine. Yet now? I don't know that I can trust you either."

Dikam tried to back up. "No, no, no," he wailed. "I don't know what's going on with your son, but I know that families can be difficult in the best of times."

At that, Austin started to laugh. "Yeah, Jake, you definitely need to transfer your shit, and you need to do it today because I don't trust anything this weasel's involved in."

"I'll sue you for defamation," Dikam declared, with a deadly tone.

"Yeah, you go for it," Austin urged him, "and then we'll talk about the documents you forged in your office." All the color left Dikam's face, and he started to shake. Austin pinned him up against the door. "So, let's take a walk down to the sheriff's office, shall we? I don't know how many of them you're paying off, but I highly doubt they will all be on your side and against Jake here."

"What the hell?" Dikam cried out. "I didn't do anything."

"No, maybe not yet, maybe not at all," Austin conceded, "but your actions are speaking a lot more clearly than your words." He looked over at Jake. "Don't worry about us, you go take care of the legals. You need to get this sorted today."

Jake nodded. "I need that paperwork."

"In that case, let's go have a talk with his secretary first, though she wasn't too friendly five minutes ago."

Jake's gaze widened. "Annalise? She's always been a sweetheart."

"I don't know who Annalise is, but the dragon I met up there was definitely not on the friendly side."

Jake snorted and headed for the front steps. Austin followed him, dragging the lawyer with him.

When they got there right behind Jake, he was snapping out orders to the Dragon Lady, as if he owned the business. The woman, on the other hand, who Jake had just called *a sweetheart*, wasn't having anything to do with it, and when she saw her boss, she stood up. "What the hell is going on here?"

Dikam winced and noted, "It seems we have an unhappy client."

She glared at him, then turned to look at Jake. "Now look. We don't have a problem here. Everything's fine."

When she caught sight of Austin, she scowled. "You," she spat.

He gave her a big fat smile. "Yeah, it's me," he said, "and you do have a problem here. I don't think your legal documents are quite legal."

She shook her head. "Everything here is on the up-and-up." She turned and looked at Jake. "Look. I don't know what this young man told you, but you obviously can't trust him. Look at him. He can't even walk in a straight line. He's probably drunk."

Jake snorted at that. "Good Christ, I have spent more than enough time with this fine young man to know when he's drunk and when he's not." He turned, looked back at the lawyer, and barked, "I'm either calling the sheriff right now, or you'll be giving me all my shit, and then I'm calling the big-town cops."

"No need to call the cops at all," Dikam stated, raising his hands. He turned to his secretary and called out, "Give him his damn files." She stared at him, wide-eyed, and shook her head. "I said, give him the files."

"You don't understand, John. Not everything is completed yet," she reminded him in a wheedling tone.

"No, I'm sure it isn't," Austin added, "but it's as complete as it'll be as far as you're concerned, and, once the authorities find out what you've been involved in, you'll be done with a lot more."

She turned and stared at him, probably wanting to spit in his face. He smiled. "Go ahead, it's not as if I haven't seen a woman lose it before."

She stiffened. "I'm not the type to lose it because of a brat like you. We're not turning over anything."

Austin just smiled, looked at Jake, and asked, "Do you

want to handle this, or shall I?"

Jake nodded at him.

Austin walked over to the nearest computer, picked up the monitor on the desk, and smashed it on the floor. Dragon Lady instantly screamed at him to get out, and he just walked over to the second desk and picked up the second monitor as John now screamed at him, "Stop, just stop!"

Austin smiled. "I have no intention of stopping, so go ahead and call the sheriff. Please, call the sheriff," he urged him in a voice that was just a hair above a prayer.

Annalise nervously wrung her hands and looked over at her boss, who shook with fury. Dikam turned to Jake and said, "Call him off. We're giving you your files, all your documents," he said. "No need for this."

"*Really*?" Jake asked. "There is obviously a need for a full investigation into what is going on here and in what way you have colluded with my son as he continues to raise hell."

The woman sniffed. "It's not as if you've ever done anything for him," she snapped, "and look at how you've treated my office."

"Your office?" Jake repeated. "Are you the lawyer around here, or is he? I didn't notice your name on the door."

She flushed in fury, an emotion that Austin recognized. "She may not be the boss, but it looks to me as if maybe she's been running the place as if she were." Austin looked over at the lawyer in time to catch the look of chagrin on Dikam's face. "Interesting that you've let her have her way in all this," he noted in a mocking voice. "That works for you, *huh*?"

He glared at him. "You don't know anything."

"No, I don't know very much, that's for sure, and I'm

not exactly certain what's going on here either, but I can tell you that, whatever it is, it really stinks. But we do know that Chris is up to something criminal, and it appears that you've become a part of it."

"I'm not part of anything," Dikam spat.

"You may have managed to hide your tracks," Austin suggested, "but that doesn't mean you've hidden everything. Believe me that it will come down to just how good of a job you've done in keeping this a secret."

At that, Annalise chimed in, "We haven't done anything wrong, and you've got no business terrorizing the place."

"Really? You have a client here looking for assistance, and you've refused to comply with his wishes. Jake should just talk to the nearest police commissioner and see how that works out for you and Dikam."

"Police commissioner?" Dikam asked. "Why not the sheriff?"

"Because we can't be sure that you aren't colluding with the sheriff, now can we?" Austin replied, with a hard smile on his face. "Do you think we haven't dealt with criminals before?"

"Now look," Dikam began, raising his hand again. "Obviously there has been some misunderstanding. I did direct my secretary to provide everything that you needed," he said in exasperation. "I'm being cooperative."

"Yeah, but she isn't."

She finally walked over to the desk that still had a computer monitor on it, where she sat down and started to print out Jake's documents.

"Put every single file of Jake's on this too," Austin ordered, handing over a USB key. She frowned, and he nodded. "Right now, while we're standing here."

"What good will that do? Obviously we'll still have records."

"Thank you for admitting that," he said, with a smile. "Pull out the physical files too. Then the electronic files will help us to know when there's a leak or when something goes wrong. That way we can determine who had access to the information in question and what they might have done with it, including anyone they may have shared this confidential information with."

She flushed, then glanced nervously over at her boss, and started transferring digital files. When she handed the thumb drive back to Austin, he passed it over to Jake. "Now, get over to your new lawyer."

Jake looked at him curiously. "What about you? Aren't you coming with me?"

"Nope, I'll stay until I get the rest of the information I want. I'll make their lives miserable, until I know that you're safe and sound and everything has been transferred over nice and legal, so that you are assured that your will still says what you think it does. Then you'll take a digital copy of all this, and we'll send it off for forensic analysis."

With a nod, Jake took off.

"What are you talking about?" John Dikam asked in shock.

"You heard exactly what I said," Austin stated, as he turned to him and smiled.

"No, no, no, there's no need for any of this," Dikam pleaded. "We haven't done anything wrong."

Jake looked at him and growled. "You sure as hell haven't done anything right, and that's where we'll start."

And, with that, the Dragon Lady gave Austin a collection of file folders. Then Austin turned and walked out.

CHAPTER 7

R OX SAT NERVOUSLY at home, busying herself with chores as she waited for somebody to come home. Her father had torn out of the place as if a fire was happening somewhere. Her mother stood here, watching nervously, wondering what the hell was going on and how things had gotten so ugly so quickly.

"What the hell did I ever do?" her mother murmured.

"I could list a few things," Rox quipped, with half a laugh, "but it wouldn't be fair to you."

"Oh, it's very fair," she muttered. "I've made plenty of mistakes."

"You're not the only one. I should never have chased away Austin."

"No, maybe not, but, if you have anything between you two that's still worth fighting for, … you might want to fight for him now."

Rox looked sideways at her mother. "You still really like him, don't you?"

"Of course I do," she stated. "He reminds me a lot of Jake. Austin is cut from the same cloth. They're hard men, but they're good, and they're there for you when you need it, whether you deserve it or not."

"So why in the hell did I get so upset?"

"Because you were probably jealous and emotional, just

wanting him to stay home and to choose you over the military," she suggested. "I think that would always be a dead end for you."

"And for him."

"But you knew it when you married him. Austin was always the same, and you changed your expectations, not him. He is still the same man he always was."

"I know. I know," she muttered. "I knew it, even back then, but I didn't really think about it."

"I think that's marriage in many ways, especially when you're young. You marry, thinking it'll all be peachy, and then you find out it's not perfect. Everything you thought would come to pass doesn't, … and you don't know how to handle it."

"Yet should he have to handle it?"

"I don't know. … It shouldn't have to be something that he feels he has to handle either. I'm not sure what he did to set you off. I just know that, for a man like him, once you give him an ultimatum, it's pretty hard to go backward."

"I never thought he would really leave," Rox wailed, sadness evident in her tone. "It never occurred to me that, from one day to the next, it could be over. I still can't believe it, to be honest."

"Maybe he was expecting you to contact him with an apology," she noted. "Did you ever think about that?"

"I did, and believe me, if I thought I could do that and he would come back, I would have done it, but I didn't even know how to get a hold of him."

"Did you try?"

"No, I didn't because … I … No, I didn't try. I was hurt. I was angry, and it just seemed like, if he wanted to leave then, what the hell? He should just leave."

"And he did exactly what you thought he would do. He left. You gave him an ultimatum, and he called your bluff."

"He also told me that he wasn't up for games, that he'd always been honest with me, and that he expected honesty from me back," she shared, "but apparently I didn't even give him that."

"In what way?" her mom asked curiously.

"Because he told me before we married that he was staying in the military, and I knew that about him. I told him that it was fine with me, as long as he came back at some point in time and stayed. I told him it was fine, that I knew he was doing what he felt he had to do, but I didn't really mean it. I just thought that, once we were together, he would be so happy with our lives that he would quit the military and would want to stay."

Amie nodded. "I think a lot of women have probably made that same mistake over the years. You can't really understand why the men feel that calling," she explained, "but it's hard for them to walk away from what they consider their duty, and, when it's duty to the family, we don't want them to ever walk away. Not when it's something like this."

"I was lonely and twenty," Rox admitted, "and more immature than I would really care to admit. And since he's been back, I've come to realize that I was also quite jealous of his relationship with Dad. At first, I thought that maybe with Austin gone, Dad and I would get closer, but instead because I'd chased Austin away, … Dad got really angry."

Amie smiled sadly. "It was really hard for him because we had invested all our love and affection into that relationship too. … When you threw it all away, … we had no say in it. And Austin never contacted us again, probably assuming that we would be on your side of the deal," Amie looked distraught just speaking about it. "There shouldn't be sides, but a divorce, a breakup like that, it's debilitating for everybody, so we also took the brunt of the breakup."

Rox nodded. "I know, and I just didn't know what to do about it."

"What do you want to do about it now? Do you like the man he's become?"

She smiled. "The thing is, he's become what I always thought he would be. It's just … It breaks my heart to know that I'm not a part of his life anymore."

"And yet he's here," Amie pointed out. "Austin didn't have to come after that dog. He could have chosen to go somewhere else, to deal with another lost War Dog in another place, but he's here."

"I think he's here to find closure," Rox suggested.

Amie went silent for a moment and nodded. "That's possible. He needs to move on too. Neither of you have moved to file for divorce in all these years, so maybe it's time. One way or another, either you call it quits or you find a way to make it work and go forward somehow," Amie said, with a searching gaze. "We've learned a lot through it ourselves," Amie noted, "and it helped us get through a time that was difficult in our own lives."

She looked at her mom in surprise. "I didn't know about that."

"No, but it came back to your father wanting a son and having a daughter," she replied, with a smile. "I always felt guilty because I never gave him what he so desperately wanted, and he always felt guilty for wanting something he knew I couldn't give him."

Rox snorted. "If there's anything more convoluted than the human psyche, I don't know what it is," she muttered.

Her mother nodded. "Anyway, it made us stronger, once we got through it, but we also had to sit beside you and watch you go to pieces, and that was incredibly hard too."

"I can imagine."

"It's one of the reasons Jake gradually became more considerate toward you. He did reach out more, and that's why you've been closer these last few years. Plus, he respected that you really do love this ranch and intend to stay and work it," she added, with a smile. "So, if there was a reason for Austin's leaving, you at least made good use of the time that he was gone. However, now if you have anything still within you that wants to make something of his return, this would be a really good time to do it."

Amie patted her daughter on the shoulder and added, "Remember that nothing is easy about love, even in the best of circumstances. It doesn't matter who it is, relationships are just plain hard." And, with that, she turned and walked upstairs.

Feeling as if once again she had major life lessons ahead of her, Rox headed out to the barn. There she found Charlie, stomping his feet anxiously, which wasn't a normal behavior for him. "You want to go for a run, buddy?" she asked him.

He snorted heavily.

"Fine, let's go. I'm not sure what's bothering you, but we'll get to it." She'd seen animals react in some of the weirdest ways, and over time she had learned not to ever ignore it. "Let's go. I'm not sure what's bothering you, but let's find out."

Rox quickly threw a saddle on him and headed out, after texting her mom to let her know what she was up to. As soon as she was out a little farther away from the house, she gave Charlie his head and let him take her where he wanted to go. Something was still bothering him, but she just didn't know what. As far as she was concerned, he would know better than her. Willing to trust him, she patted the rifle across the front of her saddle and let him go.

AFTER THE CONFRONTATION that never seemed to end, Austin decided that after dropping off the files to Jake's new lawyer, he would head out to one of the spots on the highway where he could walk into the wooded area where the War Dog had been before he disappeared. He couldn't quite make up his mind as to whether Cowboy had anything to do with this mess with Chris or not. Again Austin would hate to think that Chris had become such an ass that an animal's life was something he would exploit to hurt somebody else, but Austin had met an awful lot of jerks in his life. So just no telling who would turn out to be a jerk until things started happening. Then you were left to just stare at them, wondering how they could possibly have ended up that way.

He parked on the side of the highway and headed into the wooded area, adjacent to one of the big pastures on the other side. As he walked, he stopped several times to look around. There were no huts, no sheds, no man-made hideouts anywhere. As he kept walking, he thought he heard something in the distance, but it was faint and hard to hear anything clearly. He headed in that direction, unsure what exactly he would encounter, but he knew something—or someone—was out there.

As he walked closer, he heard a woman's voice. He picked up the pace, and, as he came around a group of trees, he saw Rox and Charlie standing there, staring off into the distance. He called out so he didn't scare her. Startled, she turned, saw him, and waved him over. He walked closer, stepping up to Charlie, who was obviously nervous and prancing around side to side. "Hey, buddy. What's going on?" He looked over at Rox. "What's the matter? Is anything wrong?"

"I don't know. Charlie was really upset back at the ranch, so I decided to ride him out to wherever he wanted to go and to see what was going on, and this is where he came. I just know that Charlie has been very intuitive at times."

"You're right. He's always been very intuitive." Austin nodded. "What is it that you're seeing though?"

"Nothing, at least nothing that makes any sense."

Just then Charlie lifted his head, nickered loudly, and bolted, jerking the lead rope from her hands, and quickly disappeared down the path.

"Shit," she muttered in astonishment. "Wow, I don't know what to say. I've never seen him do anything like that before."

"No, neither have I. Come on. Let's go after him."

"You know how fast he is. We'll never catch up with him."

"I do, but I don't think he's going far. Something up there is bothering him, and we need to sort that out, first and foremost. Maybe after that we'll even get a few more answers," he said, with a laugh.

"You think so?"

"Not really, but it's possible, so let's go see."

CHAPTER 8

TOGETHER ROX AND Austin raced after the horse.

A few minutes later Austin tugged Rox tight up against him. "Listen," he whispered.

She tilted her head, straining to hear what he'd picked up. He'd always had phenomenal hearing, leaving her with what she thought of as her great hearing in the dust. And there it was, … a faint bark. Her eyes opened wide, she stared at him, excitement evident in her expression. "You think that's Cowboy?"

"I don't know, but Charlie obviously picked up on something, and that's what we need to follow up on. However, we don't know whether they're alone." Hearing those words made her halt and stare at him, shocked. He looked at her and nodded. "Let's just go slow and be as quiet as we can."

Together, they walked, keeping an eye on the world around them and looking for anything that would explain what was up ahead. He turned to her and asked, "Did you have a rifle on your saddle?"

"It's tied up crosswise, yes. I wasn't exactly looking for trouble, but I always bring one."

The problem is, when you weren't looking for trouble is often when you found it. She also knew better than to leave it on her horse because, if anybody up there got a hold of

Charlie, her weapon was right there for the taking. With that in mind, she picked up the pace just enough to let Austin know that she was beyond concerned, but he held her back just enough that she couldn't race forward.

She glared at him, and he nodded. "I know. You want to charge into battle, but let's ensure there even is a battle first."

"What else could there be?"

"I'm not sure because I don't know what happened to Cowboy in the first place," he said, "and that is something that concerns me."

He'd always been the kind of guy who was not overly cautious but very realistic about what was out there in the world. He moved forward a few more steps, then he slowed again.

"Now what?" she asked.

"I don't like anything about this," he whispered.

"If they'll hurt Charlie or Cowboy, or if they have another dog, we need to rescue them."

"I know. I understand what you're saying, but I'm just telling you that something is off about this, and I don't like anything about it."

She nodded. "You're saying exactly what Dad and I have been saying for a while. *Something's off, and we don't know why. We don't know who,* and we haven't been able to figure it out," she shared in frustration, "and believe me, ... that's been pissing us both off." She looked over at him. "Do you really think it could be Chris?"

"I hope not," he said, "because that would be a whole new low for him, ... down more than I would ever want to see him fall, but we also know that we have very little control over somebody who's as angry as Chris is."

"I'm still not sure why he's so angry though. It's not as if we didn't talk about the ranch passing down on Jake's side of the family the whole time we were growing up. Chris knew. All along he knew."

"Knew what though?"

"He knew that he would get a share in the place, but not how much or what exactly he would get. He was always considered to be family, and it was clear there was always a place for him here."

"But not quite the same as you."

"Maybe not," she said, "but that's not my fault."

"Nope, it isn't, but Chris also might not give a crap about whose fault it is as long as he could lay the blame on somebody."

She nodded because of course she'd considered that more than a few times herself. "It's frustrating that he treats Mom and Dad that way though," she shared. "They've done nothing but be good to him."

"I wonder about his biological father though."

"I don't know much about him," she replied, with a shrug. "Mom's never really been open about him."

"That's one of the reasons I want to know more. It's one of those potential surprise elements that I'm not happy about."

She snorted. "Yeah, you want everything locked down and confirmed, don't you?"

He glanced at her sideways and asked, "Don't you?"

She flushed at that comment. As they walked forward, she added, "I never expected to see you here again, you know?"

"I'm not sure I expected that either, but a good friend of mine suggested I come and find a way to make amends or at least find closure, so I could move on."

Her heart sank at that. Of course that's exactly what she needed to do too, but she really didn't want the reminder that they should be moving on. It was hard to move on when your heart was still stuck with that one person, the one you still loved, and, in these moments, it hit her between the eyes all over again. She'd never really gotten over him, and she'd never pursued a divorce because she still loved him. She groaned out loud, and, when he looked at her, she shrugged and said, "It's nothing."

"It's obviously something."

"It's nothing I'll share," she snapped. He didn't say anything, just continued to walk forward, and, she felt terrible. He could always bring out the worst in her, and she didn't know why. Without even giving herself a moment to think or to change her mind about it, she asked him about it.

"I bring out the worst in you?" he repeated in wonder, staring at her, one eyebrow raised. "That's not good," he said. "Generally relationships are supposed to bring out the best in each other."

"Yeah, generally," she agreed, "but it never seems to work that way."

He gave her a sideways glance, "Any idea why?"

"No idea at all. If I knew, I wouldn't have asked you." He snorted at that, and she groaned. "See? I did it again. Normally I would talk like a *not-crazy* person right now."

At that, he laughed. "You're not crazy," he declared, "but I do understand. Conversation between us isn't comfortable right now, which isn't surprising, considering our history."

"Do you? Understand, I mean. I'm the one who sent you away. I'm the one who took the crap for everything I did and paid the price for everybody being pissed off at me over it," she shared, her voice rising with each phrase, and then she huffed. "Whereas, you on the other hand, didn't have to deal with any of it."

"Not true," he replied, shaking his head. "I still had to deal with the loss, the guilt of walking away, not just from you, but from two other people I cared about very deeply and knew I was hurting them as well. There were all kinds of issues, not just the ones you had to deal with. We all dealt with the fallout, including your parents."

"I know," she muttered, as she stared out at the world, as they kept walking, talking quietly on the way. "It never occurred to me that this would even happen."

"What do you mean?"

"I didn't think for a minute that you would stay away," she admitted, trying to keep the tears at bay. "I was angry, furious really, and yes, I ordered you to get lost and to never come back and all that, but it never occurred to me that you would do it."

He shot her a hard glance. "How could you not? I haven't changed. I've always been one who wouldn't play head games or deal with ultimatums. And, … for the record, … that hasn't changed."

"I know," she muttered. "I can see that. Looking back, a lot of it was just plain jealousy, just being young and stupid."

"More than that apparently," he noted, with a groan. "It seems as if you were also very insecure, and for that I would have to take some of the blame." She stopped, frowned at him, as he just shrugged and moved her forward. "Come on. We have things to do up here."

She laughed. "I know, but you caught me by surprise. I think that's the first I've ever heard you say anything about that."

"It's also the first time we're talking about it," he pointed out, "and whether it's a good talk or a bad talk isn't the issue, as long as we're communicating. As for how far it goes, I don't know. We may not agree with a lot of what we each have to say because we both think we took the brunt of it, but hopefully we're all a lot older and a lot wiser."

"I hope so too," she whispered, "but it sure doesn't feel that way."

"I'm sure it doesn't," he said. "Nothing quite like knowing that you've done something that affects everybody, only to find out that maybe it's not what you really wanted in the first place."

"I didn't even get a chance to take it back, did I?"

"Nope. You were pretty clear about what you wanted."

"I know," she said sadly. "It was one of those days, and I just lost it."

"It was one of those days, and, when you lost it, I left on a mission."

"And you didn't come back."

"Of course not," he declared, giving her a hard glance. "I didn't come back because you made things pretty clear."

"I know I did," she said in exasperation.

"And it's not as if you had done that before, so I took it to heart, and I left."

At that, they came to a clearing. He stopped, pointed a finger to the far corner, and then whispered, "Stay quiet. I'll circle around and come back."

She watched as he headed off to the side, moving silently. It was an eerie feeling knowing that he was heading into something that could be very dangerous, yet she was standing here and doing nothing.

It was almost a repeat of everything she'd gone through

before. There was something so very capable about him, which she loved, yet at the same time she hated it. Knowing that she probably hated it out of jealousy made her feel even more like a fool. She had no idea how to quantify it all.

He'd been so good at so many things, and, even though she'd been born here, had grown up here, he'd taken to it like a duck takes to water and seemed to run circles around her. Her father had even taken to him, and Jake was notoriously against everybody in her world, mostly because her father loved her so much and wanted to see her with somebody serious and good, though she didn't realize that at the time. Naturally, when she'd found Austin, they'd all been thrilled, until she sent him away. Then it had been one recrimination after another, until she'd told them to stop it or she was leaving too. Another ultimatum.

They had stopped lashing out at her, and those conversations about Austin had died instantly, and she'd been left to mull over the choice that she'd made alone. Now with Austin right here in front of her, it just seemed as if those choices had been magnified, almost as if the universe was asking if she was happy with the choices she had made, and were they choices she wanted to keep making?

Of course the answer was hell no. She definitely did not want to keep making ultimatums. She just didn't think she had any other option at the moment with Austin. That he was here helping them out right now was huge, that he'd only arrived because of the War Dog, was much harder to come to terms with, but it's not as if she'd given him much leeway to come back to talk to her. She'd told him to disappear and to never come back, and, well, … as much as she hated to say it, he'd done precisely that.

AS AUSTIN SLIPPED up to a large tree around the side, he saw Charlie dancing just out of range of some stranger trying to grab his lead rope. Seeing the scene happening in front of him, Austin whistled, and Charlie backed up.

"Whoa, whoa, whoa," the other man called out, "get over here."

Charlie danced just far enough away to stay out of his reach.

Austin whistled again, letting Charlie know he was here, hoping Charlie remembered who Austin was in terms of which man the horse should listen to. When a second whistle filled the air, he realized that Rox had heard and was calling out to him too. Charlie stepped back a little bit from the man who was getting too close, but Charlie was kind of penned in. It wasn't that there was a pen per se, but a couple other men were here too.

Austin stepped forward with a strong limp and called out, "Whoa, Charlie. It's okay, buddy." Charlie started to nicker in response.

The other men turned to look at the intruder and glared. One of them stepped forward. "Who the hell are you?"

Austin stared at him and replied, "I work here." Then he frowned. "Who the hell are you?" It wasn't anyone he knew. The leader of this trio was older, a little rougher, and looked as if life hadn't been all that easy for him the last many years. He was probably in his fifties or maybe sixties. The other two men with him didn't look terribly comfortable right now. Austin stepped into the ring that the three men had made, and Charlie moved over to him.

Austin stroked his nose. "Hey, buddy. It's okay." Austin

looked over at the men. "He doesn't know you, so he's very unsure."

One of the men turned and looked around at the other guy. "Time to go."

That man glared at him and snapped. "Not time to go yet."

The first man shrugged. "It is for me," he declared, as he started to back up.

"Any particular reason you're leaving?" Austin asked, looking at him closely. "Where's the dog?" he asked casually. "We heard it bark."

"Didn't hear no dog," he snapped. "We didn't hear nothing."

"It was pretty hard to miss," Austin stated, with a smile, "unless you've got your hearing aid turned off." The other man glared at him, and Austin nodded. "I can see you don't like anybody questioning what the hell's going on here, but the truth of the matter is, you're on private property. So you three are trespassing, and I really want to know what the hell you're up to here."

"None of your business," the main man snapped, as he backed away. He looked over at his partner and added, "I told you we need to get out of here."

His partner hesitated, as if he wasn't at all happy about the whole situation, but then finally nodded begrudgingly. "Fine, we'll just come back later."

"You might," Austin replied, "but, if you're up to no good, don't bother."

He laughed. "Like what you say has anything to do with it."

"Maybe not to you, but it's not as if I'm here alone."

Immediately the man stiffened and looked around.

Austin continued. "Do you really expect to be on private property and causing whatever trouble you're thinking of without some pushback?"

The older man glared at him. "We're not on private property."

"Oh, you sure are," Austin declared. "You're on Jake's ranch, and you know it. There are signs all over the place, and you didn't get here by chance." Just something about him seemed familiar, but not. Austin looked over at the other man, who had been trying to flee the whole time. "And what's your excuse?" The man just glared at him, and Austin nodded. "So, unless this is something I need to call the sheriff about, I suggest you disappear."

"Why would you even call the sheriff? We're just walking here."

"No, you're not," Austin snapped. "You don't just walk around on private ranchland."

The other man glared. "Nobody should own this much land," he snapped. "He doesn't need it all."

"That's beside the point, but he sure does own and need this land. Fun fact, every head of cattle requires a certain amount of land, so unless you're one of those people who don't eat beef, Jake needs what he needs," Austin shared, simple and casual. "And besides, it's his and has been in his family for a very long time. You obviously don't understand what it costs a rancher or a farmer to raise the things you consume, or you wouldn't be sitting here, mocking him for having the land he does. And, by the way, if you're thinking of stealing any beef, that's still quite a serious offense in the state of Texas."

The other man laughed. "Those are ancient laws, and nobody ever uses them."

"I wouldn't really count on that, not with all the guns people in Texas have," he added, with half a smile. With Charlie at his side, he quickly swung up onto his back, patting the horse on the neck. "You sure got him riled some. What I want to know is what the hell are you trying to do, and where the hell is that dog?"

The men all started fidgeting, looking at each other, starting to back away to where the highway would eventually meet up with them.

"We're just leaving," the third one finally said, speaking up. "We just came out for a walk, and obviously we didn't realize it was private property."

"That's a load of bull," Austin argued, as he watched them. "No way you couldn't have known. All this area is private land and posted as such. Did you see any signs of state parks or other government lands?"

"No, of course not," he snapped.

But the men continued to back up, and Austin let them. It was important to know just what the hell they were up to, if they even had any idea themselves. This was more BS than Austin expected, but, hey, they would get to the bottom of this at some point in time, at least he hoped so.

The two men continued to back away, but the old guy suddenly lunged at Charlie and made a grab for the rifle. Charlie reared up on his back legs, and it was all Austin could do to keep his seat, as the horse fought against his own fright from the old man making the sudden lunge.

Austin glared at him. "What the hell was that shit?"

The old man just glared right back at him. "I want the rifle on his back."

"That's nice, but you're not getting it." Austin patted it carefully. "Unless you want to get shot right where you stand," he added.

The old man glared at him. "You ain't nothing but a cowboy," he snapped. "You won't shoot me."

Austin gave him half a smile. "Mister, I just finished two tours overseas," he shared and finished with a smirk. "I don't give a shit about what you want. I'll drop you without a thought if I need to, so you best not ever try to take anything off me again."

With that the older man's eyes widened, as he realized he was tangling with someone with military experience. Then he just glared at him. "That ain't cool. You shouldn't even be out here. You've probably got PTSD or something."

"Doesn't matter what I got or what I don't," he replied. "It's none of your fucking business, but right now you're pissing me off. I suggest you get the hell off this land before I call the authorities, or, better yet, I'll call in Jake."

At that, the older man's lips curled. "Yeah, you do that. He's been nothing but a pain in my ass for a long time." At that, he turned and strode off, following the other two men who were already hightailing it back to the highway.

Austin let out another whistle, only to hear a response right behind him. He turned to see Rox coming up close behind Charlie, who turned ever-so-slightly and nickered at her. She sighed when she got there and pulled his head down to cuddle him. "Why the hell did you take off like that, buddy?"

"I think it was Cowboy barking," Austin suggested, with a thoughtful look. "How close were he and Cowboy?"

She frowned at him, turning to look around the area where they stood. "They were really close. Do you really think Cowboy's out here?"

"I definitely heard a dog," Austin stated, shaking his

head. "I can't tell you how, why, or where. I just know I heard a dog."

"I did too," she noted, "but not until you pointed it out."

He smiled. "And that's okay too."

"You always had that bloody superior hearing."

He shrugged. "I hope I didn't lose most of it in the accident, but who knows?"

"You never did tell us what the accident was," she noted, stroking Charlie's long forehead.

"No, I sure didn't, and I'm not explaining it now either." She frowned at him, and he frowned right back. "Now, if you're done questioning my history, let's look for Cowboy. He has to be around here somewhere."

"I've looked out here time and time again."

"Did he have any whistle or any birdcall or anything he would respond to?"

She turned and gave several short sharp whistles, but no dog came running. He tried several whistles he had heard trainers use in the military, but still, no dog bark in reply. "I just seems, if he could have come, he would have," she murmured.

"And that means that he couldn't come," Austin said. "You've got acres and acres of land here. We should have two horses or two four-wheelers," he noted, as he looked around, "so we could cover more land."

"Maybe, but if you heard Cowboy barking, that means he's alive, somebody's keeping him alive, and he can't come home. And if it was him that I saw that night, he should have been able to come home."

"You don't know who he was with though, whether he was on a tether or not," Austin pointed out. "So let's just give him a chance first."

"I've given him many chances," she wailed. "I just want him home, safe and sound."

"Which would be the ideal, but, in order to have that happen, we have to find him. I'm pretty damn sure he's out here somewhere." Just then he tilted his head again and asked, "Is Charlie up to carrying both of us?"

She laughed. "He always used to be, and he's not that old." And, with that, using his foot for support, she swung up to sit behind the saddle.

"Not very comfortable for you though," he noted, twisting to look at her. "Are you okay?"

"I'm okay if we're not going too far, but we'll need to keep it short for Charlie's sake."

"Let's go up a little bit and take a look," he suggested, "because I just heard a dog."

And with that, they moved out, Charlie never once grimacing over the extra weight. By the time he got them up to the area he thought the barking was coming from, he said, "Hop down and let's go take a closer look."

"Take a look at what?" she asked, not sure what they were supposed to do.

He frowned at her in astonishment and pointed. "Looks to be a hunter's blind."

"There can't be any hunter's blind out here," she snapped. "This is private land."

"And since when did that ever stop anybody?"

Sure enough, she watched as he led them in one direction. She couldn't see anything, other than trees. Yet, once they got closer, she finally saw some sort of hideout underneath the tree canopy. She nodded and pointed.

He put a finger to his lips, and, stepping up to the side,

he peered in through one of the openings. Almost immediately came frenzied barking on the other side. When they stepped up closer, the barking and chaos turned into whines.

She cried out, "Cowboy, oh my God. It's Cowboy." It took a minute for them to cut through the brush to see that he'd been penned up. It wasn't very big, but it was enough that he couldn't get a running jump out, and thick enough that he couldn't climb through.

"Jesus Christ," she swore, as the two of them worked to break down the barrier that had clearly been erected to keep him there. "What the hell were these people thinking?"

"I don't think they were, except that, for whatever reason, keeping Cowboy here was either part of their plan or part of some future plan," he suggested. "I don't know what's going on here, but the sooner we find out the better."

"At least it looks like they were feeding him but probably not enough. And his water bowl is totally empty."

Once he was free, Cowboy raced around Charlie, and the two animals nuzzled each other, as Cowboy jumped back and forth in joy.

"My God," she muttered, as she dropped to her knees when Cowboy burrowed up against her, knocking her to the ground. "I've been looking and looking for you for weeks, Cowboy," she whispered. "I used to come out here every evening trying to find him. I can't believe you did it." As she fought back the tears forming in her eyes, she looked up at him and shook her head. "Thank you … really." He just nodded, and then she froze. "I suppose," she began, her tone careful, "I suppose you'll be leaving now."

He shook his head. "No, not yet."

"But finding Cowboy is what you came for."

"I came to ensure he was okay and to confirm he was

loved and well cared for," he clarified, "but obviously still some questions remain."

She winced at that. "Now I suppose you'll tell me that I'm not a good-enough dog mom to keep him."

"No, I didn't say that at all," he replied in a mild tone, "so don't go putting words in my mouth."

She glared at him, then hopped back up on her feet, reaching a hand down to Cowboy, but he kept barking and nudging her. She frowned, then realized that Austin was right.

"Something's wrong," Austin noted, looking around. "Cowboy was being kept here for a reason, and what we don't know is what else is going on."

"Yeah, something is up," she muttered. "This is bizarre behavior for him."

"Which just means that it's very important," Austin said. "Anything out of the norm is something we need to know about right now. Let's put a lead on him." Then he asked her, "Is he normally leashed?"

She shook her head. "No, I've never really needed to."

"In that case, just let Cowboy run, and see what he does."

She stepped back and smiled at the War Dog. "Go ahead, Cowboy. Show us what's going on."

He looked at her, cocked his head, then barked once and took off deeper into the trees. They followed, leading Charlie behind them. When they got farther in, she frowned at Austin and added, "I almost never come into this area. I can't even remember the last time I was here."

"And that's important too," Austin noted, "because something is going on here, and it seems to involve this spot."

They kept walking deeper and deeper into the vegetation, with Cowboy continuously looking back to ensure they were coming. "We're here. It's okay, boy. Keep going. We're coming with you." He barked several more times, raced ahead a little bit, and then waited for them to catch up.

"He's really determined that we be a part of this," she muttered.

"He's determined that we need to see whatever it is that he thinks is so important." As soon as they got farther up to one area, he stopped and barked.

But she saw nothing. She looked over at Austin. "I don't know what's wrong here, but it seems as if something is, at least to Cowboy."

Austin nodded. "He has a pretty good idea that something is up." He handed her the lead rope for Charlie. "Stay here."

He moved forward several feet away, but she could see him. Then, just like, that he disappeared from view.

AUSTIN DIDN'T SEE the blind, coming out of nowhere. So, when he tripped on it, his weight came down onto a weak corner of whatever was underneath, he fell straight in. It wasn't very far, wasn't very deep, and for that he was grateful because his leg twisted partly underneath him. Swearing, he got back to his feet, hobbling ever-so-slightly as he looked around. He called out, "I'm fine, by the way."

"Jesus," she muttered, peering over into the hole. "Are you sure?"

"I am. You don't happen to have a flashlight, do you?"

When she shook her head, he pulled out his phone, put

it on Flashlight mode, then looked around, giving a whistle. "That's interesting," he said, calling out loud to her.

"What is it?" she cried out.

He took several photos and looked up at her. "It's a stash of guns. … Drugs might be in here too."

"What?" she asked, alarmed. She tried to peer over into the hole, but he shook his head. "Whatever you do, don't come closer. We'll have enough trouble getting me out of here as it is." When she frowned at him, he shrugged. "Not sure the prosthetic will like this much."

"Oh crap," she muttered. "I didn't even think about it."

"And don't think about it now either," he snapped. "I'll be fine." Although he wasn't exactly sure what *fine* would mean in this instance. "Call your father and get him headed out here now."

She stepped back ever-so-slightly and made the call. Austin heard the one-sided conversation and the urgency in her tone. When she was done, he called out, "Now call the sheriff."

"Are you sure? I want my father to see this first."

He hesitated, then nodded, but, not wanting to take any chances, he sent several of the photos to Badger. Austin took a second look, wondering how the hell he was supposed to get out of this hole. Circling his phone's flashlight around the blind, Austin located a couple steps cutting into one side, as if that was the route someone had used before. So, as he managed to swing himself partly up, Rox reached down and grabbed his belt and hauled him farther up to the top. He rolled onto the ground on his back, then looked up and smiled. "Thanks."

She grinned at him. "No problem. As I recall, we used to do things like that all the time."

"We did," he agreed, with a nod. "Nice to know you haven't forgotten."

She stepped back, feeling a little self-conscious, adding softly, "I don't think I've forgotten anything."

He stared up at her, not moving from where he lay on the ground. "What makes you think I have?"

She glared at him. "Because you never came back."

"And you never said you were sorry or that you didn't mean it."

She blinked at him several times and shook her head. "Are you telling me that you would have come back if I had?"

"I'm not sure," he admitted. "I never got the chance to figure it out, but I sure wouldn't come back without it."

"Stubborn," she snapped.

He grinned at her. "Look who's talking." It wasn't long before they heard the sound of a four-wheeler, racing toward them. "I hope that's a friendly coming at us. Does your dad drive one of those?"

"Only under duress," she muttered, "but this might qualify."

"Or it could also be somebody else," Austin noted. "So let's take the prudent course and step back into hiding."

She quickly nodded, then pulled Charlie farther back out of view, at least for the initial go-round. As soon as she did that, she called out and added, "Don't you be a hero either."

"No," he replied, "my hero days are over."

"Are you sure? Because at one point in time, you weren't ever going to quit."

"I would quit eventually," he admitted, just loud enough that she could hear. "It's just that my timing wasn't your timing."

"I don't think your timing was ever my timing," she muttered. "If I had had my way, you never would have gone back out again."

"No, and I would have been a lesser man for it."

"And you also would have been whole," she pointed out. "I don't know when you were injured, since you won't talk about it, but at least you would have been home in one piece."

"Maybe," he conceded, "but that was a lesser consequence than doing what I felt was my duty to do."

"You always were stubborn that way."

"So were you," he stated. "Didn't we just have that conversation?"

The four-wheeler broke into view, and Jake roared up to them, glaring. "What the hell is going on out here?"

Austin sat up and motioned toward the hole in the ground. "You need to take a look at this."

He glanced around the area and frowned. "We're rarely here. This is just one of the familiar haunts for the cows when it gets hot, but it's an area where we don't have any trouble."

Austin groaned. "That may have been true, … until now."

Jake hopped off the four-wheeler and, without another thought, jumped into the hole that Austin had just come out of. Seconds later, he swore at the top of his lungs. "What the fucking hell is going on here?" he roared.

"Yeah, that was my reaction too," Austin replied.

Jake glared up at him. "Who the hell is running this?"

"I don't know, but I suggest we contact the authorities and get somebody in here to take control of this."

At that, Jake shook his head. "I don't want people crawling all over my land."

"Okay, but you don't want gun-runners using your place either, right? Plus, I'm pretty sure drugs are in that blind as well, although it appears to be more firearms than anything."

Jake turned around, and, instead of hopping out, he started taking photos, and Austin didn't blame him. This was one of those things where you wanted hard evidence before you called in anyone else.

Jake noted, "You know, ever since you've come back, it's been nothing but trouble around here."

Austin laughed and answered in the same tone, "Ever since I left, you guys have had nothing but trouble."

Jake frowned and shrugged. "You could be right there, son," he muttered, his tone tired. "You could be right. That doesn't say much for when you leave again."

Jake scrambled up over the ledge a whole lot easier than Austin had and sat down on the ground, just staring around him. "Where's Rox?"

"I'm right here, Dad," she replied, as she walked Charlie forward.

He nodded, looked over at Charlie, and then realized that Cowboy was here as well. His face lit up. "Oh my God. Hey, Cowboy."

The dog broke loose from the hold Rox had around his neck and raced over and jumped into the big man's lap, knocking him over.

"I can see that Cowboy's been well loved here," Austin noted, a smile on his face.

Still laughing at being knocked over, Jake snorted. "We always love dogs around this place, and this one is more of a character than many."

"Oh, I can see that," Austin agreed. "Now, what do you

want to do?"

He glared at him. "If I had my way, I'd bury this whole mess somewhere else and ensure they couldn't dig it up again."

"You also know that they would just find it, dig it out, and, if you tried to move it on them again, they'll come after you or Amie or Rox."

Jake winced at that. "I would like to set up a welcome committee for them, but the times have changed, and I can't just shoot everybody," he complained, shaking his head. "But I'm damn well more than ready to shoot anybody I find on my property now," he muttered. "This is complete bullshit."

"Oh, I'm in agreement there, but—"

Jake raised a hand to interrupt Austin. "I know. I know. I can't just wait for them to come back and gun them down."

"No, you can't," Rox confirmed in a sharp tone. "Not even if the law allowed you to."

When he just glared at her, she glared right back.

"Nice to know you guys are getting along so well," Austin teased, with a smile.

Jake continued to glare at his daughter. "She doesn't get how the world works."

"I'm not a child," she snapped. "Of course I get it." Her father opened his mouth to say something, and then thought better of it. She nodded. "That's a really good choice."

Jake just rolled his eyes and looked back over at Austin. "So, what do you think we should do?"

"I think you should bring in somebody above the local sheriff. That's not to say your sheriff is bad. I'm just saying that he'll have his hands full, and, no matter what he does, he'll have trouble. So, if you bring in authorities above him, it'll be a lot easier to deal with these gun-runners and possibly drug dealers. And, if the local sheriff *should* be involved somehow or even looking the other way, someone will be on hand to deal with it."

"Yeah, and who will that be?" Jake asked, staring at Austin. "As gun-runners go, this is not a lot," he pointed out, waving his hands. "Yet it's still a lot to be buried on my land."

"It's a lot of trouble regardless," Austin muttered. "Between thirty to sixty weapons are in there that I can easily see. No telling how many more may be buried in there," he added. "So, whether somebody is planning a shootout or making trades, I don't know."

"I think way more than sixty weapons are in there." Jake groaned. "Honest to God, it seemed as if it was a pretty bottomless well."

"I wouldn't be at all surprised. I just don't know who's involved and how long these guns have been here," Austin stated. "You also need to know about the characters we met earlier." And, with that, Rox interrupting once again, they managed to tell Jake about the three men they had encountered.

"Here on my land?" Jake roared, staring at them in astonishment, as they both nodded. "What the hell?" he snapped. "That is not okay."

"Agreed," Austin said. "Given their proximity to this weapons stash, and the fact that they were here and were fairly aggressive about it," he added, "I'm pretty damn sure that we'll find out that this is their cache, or whoever they are working for."

Jake looked over at his daughter. "Did you know them?"

She shook her head. "No, but the one looked familiar. Yet I really don't know why," she shared. "I don't think he's from town, but still I recognized something about him."

"I did too." Austin pondered in silence for a moment. "So, if we drove through town, do you think we might see him?"

She shrugged. "I couldn't say, but obviously I'll keep an eye out for him now."

He nodded at that. "I think we'll need to do more than that. We don't want these weapons getting out into the public. You guys here in Texas can buy weapons wherever the hell you want, so why are these ones stashed here? With the laws on gun possession as relaxed as they are here, it's not as if we need a cloak-and-dagger black market operation like this. So, if they are stashing them here, it's not for any good reason."

Jake stared out across his land, facing the Mexico border. "The border is not that far away, although my land doesn't reach Mexico for sure. While everyone is surely now very aware of drug smuggling going on nearby, coming back and forth, plus people coming back and forth," he added, "I just never think it'll touch our ranch. Plus, why bury this stash here? *Running*, whether drugs, guns, or people, implies moving all this along the black-market highway. And my ranch definitely is not part of the usual running route. So I don't understand why the weapons are stashed here. Why stop right here and bury all this?"

Rox asked, "When you say *people*, are you talking illegal immigrants or human trafficking?"

"Both. Absolutely," Jake interjected, "and the fact is that we have a problem with slavery, prostitution, and all kinds of stuff. There was a smuggler's trail through here at one point, but that was a very long time ago. I was pretty-darn sure we didn't have any of that happening now."

"Was that in your day?" Austin asked, frowning.

"No, that was back in my granddad's time," he clarified. "They were bringing women across from Mexico and forcing them to work in town."

"That sounds pretty ugly," Austin muttered.

"Oh, it was, and it still sounds like a nightmare. We haven't had anything like that since."

"Guess what?" Austin noted. "Seems you probably do now."

CHAPTER 9

ROX SLOWLY RODE Charlie home, leaving Cowboy behind with Austin and her dad. She couldn't think of any reason why the drugs and the guns were buried on their ranch, but that was a hell of a place to hide them. Out in the middle of nowhere, on private land, just out on the range, with nobody to disturb them but the odd cow or two. For all she knew, the gun-runners were helping themselves to a little bit of beef at the same time.

When she got back home, Amie was waiting, a frown on her face. "I don't know what's going on, but it would be nice if somebody would fill me in."

Rox winced at that, gave her mom a hug, and noted, "We found something out there." Then she smiled. "We also found Cowboy."

Amie's face lit up. "You found Cowboy, after all this time?"

She nodded. "I think somebody was using him to keep an eye on a stash of weapons."

At that, all the color fled from her mother's face. "What do you mean, a stash of weapons?" she asked, her hand going to her chest.

Rox told her about Austin basically falling in the pit and finding the weapons there.

"That's insane," Amie muttered, disbelief in her gaze.

"Anybody would know that's Jake's land, and he won't tolerate that. Why would anybody hide them way out there in the middle of nowhere?" she asked, and then shook her head. "There's got to be better, more convenient places to stash weapons."

"But, if you think about it, the road runs by not too far from there," Rox pointed out, "so it makes some sense."

"None of it makes sense," she muttered, frowning at her daughter. "How could any of this make sense?"

"What if this stash of goods is meant for someone local?" Rox suggested, giving her mother another quick hug. "I'm putting on coffee, but I'm not sure how long they'll be or even what the next step is."

"What do you mean? Surely they'll call the sheriff."

"Austin wanted to avoid the local authorities and go one level above. Yet I'm not sure Dad is up for calling in the cavalry at all," she replied. "I think he's pissed off enough right now that he wants to move the guns, taking them away from the people who used his land to stash them. You know, a finders-keepers thing, seeing as how it's his land anyway, and meanwhile, run down whoever is poaching on his land."

"Are they poaching though?" Amie asked.

"I don't know," Rox admitted, with a wave of her hand. "No doubt we're down a head or two, but we're certainly not down more than what looks to be personal use."

"Right," Amie muttered, reaching up a shaky hand, "but that's not very helpful."

Rox snorted. "Have you seen anything in this that's helpful?"

"Yes," she declared. "Austin."

Rox winced at that and then slowly nodded. "I will admit he's been very handy to have around again."

"Handy enough to figure out if you can make peace with him?" her mother asked.

Rox shrugged. "I definitely intend to make peace with him, if only for my own peace of mind—but that doesn't mean we're getting back together again," she warned her mother. Amie's face fell, letting Rox know that's exactly what her mom was hoping for.

"Why not?" her mother asked. "It's obvious you two still care about each other."

"Maybe, though I don't know about him. I'm not sure I even still know him. I care about him, sure, but then I never stopped caring," she added, unable to give a coherent response. "All that doesn't mean he wants to hook up with a child again either."

"You're not a child," Amie declared.

"No, but what I did was childish and foolish," she admitted, "and I caused a lot of pain for all of you. I don't want to go there again."

"Of course not, none of us want you to go there again," she said, taking her daughter's hand. "But just because you messed up, what, six years ago now …"

"Five," she clarified. "Five years, five very long years, knowing exactly how you guys felt about it."

"Yes, I remember." Amie rolled her eyes. "We didn't treat you very nicely over the decision you made regarding Austin."

"It's not so much that I even really made a decision, and I think that's the part we all had a hard time with. I was angry and kicked him out, while shooting off my mouth. I don't even remember why I was so angry."

Amie smiled a sad smile, as she faced her daughter. "You do, but maybe you just don't want to recognize it."

Rox frowned. "I wasn't pregnant though, remember?"

"We don't know that for sure," her mother replied, "although you were certainly acting hormonal enough to be pregnant."

"Yeah, sure, *great*, but acting that way doesn't give me a pass for that kind of behavior. As it turned out, … maybe I'd had a miscarriage, but it would have been extremely early on, and I don't even know for sure I was pregnant. Symptoms aside, it could have been all kinds of things."

"I know," Amie agreed. "I also know that you're quite willing to bash yourself over it all until the world ends. However, at some point in time, you have to let yourself off the hook too."

"Will you let me off the hook?" Rox asked.

Amie winced. "Yes, I absolutely will let you off the hook because life, as I know it, isn't perfect. I was pretty emotionally strung out at the time myself because we all really loved Austin. He was like a son to us, and to find out that he walked without even saying anything to us was very hard."

"Yet how could he, when I didn't even give him a chance," Rox shared bitterly. "I made sure he knew he wasn't welcome."

"Maybe," Amie conceded, "and that was tough on both of us, but it's also been a lot of years later now. Maybe both of you have changed, or maybe neither of you has changed enough to even want to move on. I don't know. I'm not holding my breath that you'll work it out, but I am hoping you each find peace in your own way. You both need it."

"He's a good man," Rox admitted, her sadness evident in her tone.

"I don't know exactly what happened with his accident, but the thought that he went through something like that alone, without us, without any support, without you, is just …" Amie shook her head, tears in her eyes. "It breaks my heart. I don't know what it would have taken for him to contact us, but a life-changing accident like that surely would have been more than he could have handled all by himself."

Maybe he did have someone to help him through, Rox thought, but she abruptly shoved that idea out of her mind. She couldn't handle that right now. Or ever.

Her mother touched her arm, bringing Rox back to the present. Rox shook her head, adding, "Of course it was hard on him. Believe me that I've thought about it a lot, and, so far, he won't tell me what happened. I haven't really pushed it hard, but you're right. Just thinking that he was hurt and lying broken somewhere, knowing that he was alone and nobody gave a shit? That is one of the hardest things for me to get past mentally. I never intended for him to leave and to never come back again," she murmured. "He has always been my heart and soul, until he just wasn't here anymore."

"There is a time for you to get past that too," Amie reminded her daughter, "and this is it. You have a chance now. He is here, and, for better or for worse, you guys need to deal with whatever emotions you have left to deal with. If you don't get back together in the end, that's fine, but at least hopefully you both get closure and can begin to move on."

"All these years that he's been gone," Rox muttered, "I never once even dated."

Her mother grimaced. "I was hoping that at least you would come to terms with the idea that what you had with Austin was something that you still wanted."

"I didn't need to go on a date for that clarity," Rox stated bluntly. "I already knew it," she murmured. "He was always that part of my heart that I could never walk away from."

"You shouldn't have to," her mother agreed. "When it's your heart, it's the heart speaking to you. You can't change it, even though you might want to. You might think you should, but it's not quite that simple."

"None of this is simple," Rox murmured. "Honest to God, it's all just heartbreaking."

Amie walked over and gave her a hug. "And yet you've grown up beautifully."

"I just wasn't grown up back then, was I?"

Amie smiled and patted her cheek gently. "You were as you always are, a beautiful young woman. You just wanted a little more from him than he was ready to give you, and your method of letting him know that you wanted more of him alienated you two. That is probably what caused the problem."

"Ya think?" Rox quipped, with a headshake. "I was spoiled rotten and definitely didn't deserve him. I totally missed the whole idea of *commitment to serve*, which is clearly so important to him. I was an immature brat, and I deserved what I got."

"No, stop now," Amie said firmly. "You don't need to go down that pathway. You grew up, you learned, you changed, and you found yourself. That can be incredibly difficult to do. Some of us never quite get there. Just look at your brother."

"Do I have to?" she asked, with a wince. "You do realize that he will probably be in the middle of this mess somehow. Oh, I almost didn't tell you." Then she quickly filled her mother in on the men they had met out there.

"What the hell were they doing there?" Amie asked in astonishment. "I've never known people to speak of your father like that. He's always been highly respected here," she noted, "and no one would dare to come onto our land like that. I'm finding this all very difficult to understand."

"Yeah, if you're finding it difficult, imagine how that's going for Dad," Rox pointed out.

Amie winced again. "No, you're right. This will shake him to the core. His word was always law, and people respected him and held on to that as part of the relationship with him, even if they disagreed on other matters," she murmured. "This will break his heart."

"It might not break his heart, but I think it'll be a tough thing for him to get past. He's always been extremely proud but fair, and somehow there seems to be a lack of respect happening in this case. I don't know if it's ..." She turned to her mother, frowning, then asked, "That land, where the guns were stashed, was it always part of Dad's family ranch?"

Her mother shrugged. "I don't know, not for sure. As far as I know it was. But you know how your father is. He's buying up land adjoining ours as often as he can."

"I just wonder if there was some dispute in the past or something, and maybe we have another family-owned-land-for-generations hating on Dad."

"Maybe, but why would that have anything to do with your brother? Chris didn't have anything to do with any of that."

"No, but I'm starting to realize how anger can make someone very impressionable and how willing you are to step out of your normal behavior and do things you wouldn't normally do just because you're so fired up about being right—or at least about being wronged and not getting what you want. In that state of anger, then you're quite happy to let other people lead you astray."

"Chris was never that weak before," Amie said, frowning, shaking her head.

"Maybe, but … I wonder if we ever really knew him. After all, I didn't even know myself for the longest time, and I still don't in many ways. I've come a long way, and I agree that I've certainly changed and grown, but I've got a lot more to go, and maybe Chris does too."

"He absolutely does, but I want to ensure that he stays alive to do it," Amie murmured. "Nothing is worse than watching your children go down a pathway that you can't follow, knowing that it's theirs to destroy or to fix. It's their future to create as they want. Yet, as parents, we are left doing nothing, other than providing words of advice and hoping they won't just throw it out the window because they fail to care anymore."

Rox studied her mother intently. "I care," she declared instantly, "but, back then, I was blind and hurt when it came to Austin. Only now have I come to realize that part of the reason I was so hurt was because I was jealous of the relationship he had with Dad."

Her mother just shook her head, as she stared at her daughter. "And that is foolish," she declared. "Your father loves you."

"Yes, but I'm not his son. I am his daughter, and, as much as I hate to admit it, that matters to him. He is my father, and I love him, but I know he really wanted a son."

Her mother's face pinched, and she slowly nodded. "Yes, it does matter because he always wanted a son. He wanted a son to carry on the legacy of the ranch. He had hopes for that, and I think, once he realized that Austin was as good of a man as he was, Jake was really proud of you and happy for you to marry Austin, plus ecstatic for himself because then he had somebody he could count on to help take the burden of the ranch, someone he could trust to do what was right."

"But Dad couldn't trust me," Rox muttered, shaking her head.

"I won't make any excuses for Jake, and I don't know that it's something you could ever understand, but I can tell you that there has always been a bloodline family member running this property. Even though your brother was rather desperate to own it, Jake didn't ever fully trust Chris."

"I don't fully trust him myself," Rox admitted bluntly. "I was always worried that Chris would end up with the controlling interest. If so, I would probably end up leaving."

Amie stared at her in shock. "Why would you leave?"

"Because I'm not sure Chris and I would get along all that well when it came to running this ranch," she clarified. "I've got decades of experience here, while Chris was avoiding anything to do with work on this ranch. So, if he had a controlling interest, then that meant he could do whatever he wanted to, with no rhyme or reason, and no one could stop him anyway. Why would I put myself through that hell?"

Amie sat down at the closest kitchen chair and just stared at her daughter. "Maybe that's what your father was always so worried about. I know that he really struggled with Chris's interest, and I tried hard to get Jake to understand where Chris was coming from. Yet, to a large degree, I didn't even understand where Chris was coming from myself. He seemed to have his own ax to grind, and it was all about the ranch. But it was never his, and, outside of joking when he was a small child, playing make believe, it was never about him getting the ranch."

"It may not have been about that from your point of view, but it could be something that Chris harbored over the years," she pointed out, with a shrug.

"He never mentioned it," Amie said, shaking her head.

She frowned and looked over at her mother. "Was there anybody else in his life who might have been pushing it?"

Amie shrugged. "I don't know. I really don't know."

Rox just nodded and let it go. What she needed was for the men to come back and to update them over exactly what the hell was going on and what they would do about it. She was afraid her father would want to hang on to the weapons, just to antagonize whoever they were dealing with, eventually bringing the fight even closer to home. That was something Rox didn't want her mother involved in.

It didn't mean that Austin would see it the same way though. Rox just needed to calm down and to wash off the dirt from the ride. As soon as she returned from a hot shower, she checked out front at the noise, seeing her father and Austin walking up the front steps. She opened the front door and asked them, "And?"

Her father looked at her irritably. "And what?" he snapped.

"No need to be snappy. This concerns all of us."

Jake nodded. "The sheriff is pissed at me because I didn't go directly to him. Some of Austin's friends contacted him, saying they were getting involved, and he's wondering why the hell I didn't let him know what was going on, and I can't say that I blame him. Hell, I didn't even know who contacted them and what they knew, so what could I say to him?" he muttered, clearly annoyed. "So ridiculous." He glared at Austin. "And you still think Chris is involved?"

"I don't know who's involved, Jake," he replied, looking over at him. "And that's the problem. We have nothing. Yet there is no avoiding a significant cache of weapons hidden on your land. If it was a much larger stash, I would be more worried, so this just makes me *worried*."

Jake stared at his son-in-law. "What the hell does *worried* mean?"

"I'm worried that there's more," he shared. "More guns, more drugs, more of whatever's out there. And it must be going to someone local. I don't know that for sure, but being off the beaten path here, I wouldn't presume this was the normal drug-running, gun-running, people-running operation passing through your land. So it would be good if we could use Cowboy to see if we can find more."

"I highly doubt Cowboy would find anything at this point in time," Amie suggested. "You would think he would be pretty traumatized by now."

"But you guys need to remember that Cowboy is a War Dog. He was trained to assist our military in war. I don't know what Cowboy's particular skills are, but I already contacted my boss and asked him to dig into that and to share that with me. For all we know, Cowboy is a bomb-sniffing dog. Plus, he did lead us right to the guns. So I think Cowboy held it together pretty well, after his weeks of captivity." Austin patted Cowboy, who had been stuck by his side since showing up to free him. Austin smiled at the War Dog and gave him a bit of a cuddle. "He's been a really good boy out there."

Jake nodded. "He did handle himself well," he admitted reluctantly, "but he's home now. So I think it's fair that he retires."

"Nobody here gets to retire until this is solved," Austin declared, giving Jake a hard glance. "You and I both know that, once these guys find out their weapons are gone, there's no guarantee they aren't coming here looking for them."

"I wish they would," Jake grumbled.

"Yes, but you're not alone," Austin snapped at him. "Two women are here, and you've got a couple ranch hands, but they're not gunmen."

"Raul is," he said, with a snort. "He can handle himself just fine."

At that, Austin stared at him and asked, "And do you trust him?"

Jake frowned. "Of course I do."

"There is no *of course* in this," Austin muttered. "Somebody had access to the property, probably repeatedly. Somebody knew how much traffic would or would not be around that area," he clarified, "so I don't really trust anybody at this point."

"*Right*," Jake muttered. "If you think there is any issue, you're welcome to question him. He won't take it kindly though."

"He might not, but surely he would understand."

"No, I'm not so sure he would." Jake looked over at his wife. "What do you think?"

"No, Raul won't understand it at all. He would take it as a lack of loyalty or belief in him on our part," she told Austin.

"Maybe," Austin noted. "I'll tailor any questions to at least find out if he's seen anybody or knows anybody who may have been coming back and forth. Your ranch may not be at the border, but your property is near enough to the border that this could be some side route, again pointing to some locals who may be involved in running these goods found on Jake's property. I don't want to make this about illegal immigrants or worse, human trafficking. I don't want to make this about anything except the fact that you now have a problem on your land, particularly with guns and drugs, it seems."

Rox asked, "So the guns were taken away? By whom?"

Jake pointed a thumb in Austin's direction. "*His* people."

Rox frowned his way, expecting more to be shared.

Austin nodded. "My boss has connections all over. He sent over a couple of FBI agents who were in the nearby area, plus a couple of retired military people he knew were here locally. One of them notified the sheriff, a courtesy call of sorts. They may need to work together on this."

"How much of a problem is it really?" Amie asked, looking at the two of them. "I heard it was sixty guns. How long do you think it's been going on? Maybe some person buys guns and buries them, ten at a time."

Austin added, "And it could just be one of many stashes on Jake's land."

At that, Jake growled. "Better the hell not be."

Austin nodded. "No way to know at this point," Austin said, looking at Amie. "If you're fine with people using your land for storing weapons and drugs, then it's not a problem at all. It wouldn't be how I would want my land to be dealt with, but it's not my place." Amie flushed in embarrassment.

At that, Jake snorted. "It was supposed to be yours, damn it." With that outburst, he got up, shoved the table out of his way, and walked off, leaving Amie and Austin and Rox staring at each other.

THAT WASN'T QUITE the reaction Austin had expected, but it gave him an insight into how pissed off and frustrated everybody was. He turned to look at Rox, one eyebrow raised. "Has that been his attitude this whole time?"

She just nodded. "Pretty much. When I disappoint people, I do it in a big way."

"That's not fair," he said. "Two of us were in that relationship, and that's who ended it," he snapped. "Nobody gets to blame just you for that."

She glared at him. "News flash, too late for that. I've already been well blamed and for quite a while now."

He just glared at her and turned to look at Amie, who shrugged.

"What do you want me to say? It was a tough time for all of us."

"Maybe so, but Rox gets to make decisions on her own too," he declared, trying to rein in his temper.

Amie nodded. "I agree. It was her decision, but it was a decision that affected all of us," Amie stated defensively, "so it is what it is." She threw up her hands. "I'll go spend some time with my husband." And she stormed off herself.

Austin shook his head, then turned to Rox. "Did you ever tell them to just mind their own business?"

She laughed. "I tried, but it didn't go over so well."

He gave her a reluctant smile. "No, your dad is a bit of a steamroller, and it's always been his way or the highway."

"It's his way, his highway, and get your ass in gear before he finds out you didn't leave on the first train," she muttered. "Believe me, if there are any issues here over the property with Chris, it's more about Dad than anything."

"I'm not even particularly thinking about that either," Austin replied, "because an awful lot is going on here."

"And yet nothing is bad enough that anybody'll take action," she pointed out. "Finding a stash of weapons? I can see Dad just wanting to hang on to them to see who comes looking for them."

"Even with you and Amie here?"

She nodded. "Yes, even with us here. He's old school, and he looks after his own," she said. "It's just that, looking after his own isn't always the easiest."

"Of course not," Austin agreed. "It's not as if he's got a dozen men here to back him up."

"No, but those he does have here are loyal."

"And that's one of the reasons I wanted to talk to Raul. Do you think he's loyal?"

She pondered that and then shrugged. "I think so, but, sure, that's something we might have to look at."

Austin left it there, and, later that night, Badger texted a list of the skills that Cowboy had. *Impressive.* Austin immediately phoned Badger, updating him and Kat, when she asked, "Are you staying?"

Only then did Austin realize that technically his job here was over. He frowned at that.

"Are you staying?" Kat asked again.

That was the question that he'd been avoiding.

She continued. "Technically the job is over. You found Cowboy, and he's doing fine."

"But I don't know who kidnapped him and who penned him up away from his family in the first place," he finally said. "It makes no sense."

"They obviously needed Cowboy to keep watch on their cache," she noted. "So what's bothering you?"

"What's bothering me is that Cowboy hasn't been here for that long of a time, so he wouldn't have gone with just anybody. So, in my head, it's an inside job."

There was silence at that, and then she sighed. "Life just

isn't quite so easy, is it?"

"No, it isn't," he murmured, "and, in this case, something feels very wrong."

"I know," she agreed. "You've mentioned that several times."

"But it's more than that. I don't know if this is just dysfunctional family stuff or something more. I haven't been here long enough to sort that out, and I was away for many years, so I see undercurrents going on here that I don't really understand. Plus, we have a very disgruntled stepson who wants nothing to do with his stepfather and appears to be more than happy to make as much trouble as he can, but hoarding guns? I don't know. I suspect that most of them were more military-grade than anything, probably bought on the black market, but it's what they're planning on doing with them that's the question."

"How many are we talking?" Badger cut in.

"I thought originally it was about forty or so, just from what I could see," he replied. "However, that underground bunker may have gone a whole lot deeper. Once that team was sent in, we were all kicked out, and the weapons were quickly removed."

"Sure, quickly removed, but …"

"Yeah, it's more likely that you can get the information we need more than I can," Austin shared, with a note of humor.

"I can make a phone call, but that doesn't mean they'll think I have any pull in that department."

"Yet you had a lot of pull when it came to getting the right people in place to handle this."

"That part was easy. However, I highly suspect your part deals very much with a family issue, and will be something that further tears apart your family."

Austin sighed. "So, two ranch hands are here, and, when I mentioned questioning them about seeing any strangers about the place, everybody got quite upset."

"Why is that?"

"Just that the ranch hands, Raul in particular, would consider any questioning to be doubting his loyalty, suggesting that Amie and Jake and Rox didn't trust Raul, even after all this time. I think they were trying to avoid that at all costs."

"Sure, but that doesn't change the fact that somebody knew the dog was involved. Somebody had to have the ability to get him to come closer. No way a stranger could have put him in that pen."

"Unless it was somebody with a military background, accustomed to dealing with War Dogs," Austin pointed out. "You and I both know that, as much as we want to think the animals are capable of discerning friend from foe, a lot of times they aren't."

"That's true," Badger agreed thoughtfully. "But these War Dogs are not stupid, and Cowboy was more than happy to come home, wasn't he?"

"Yes, very happy," Austin confirmed, "and he's in the house again. I know that Rox is particularly overjoyed that he's home."

"How are things going between the two of you?" Kat asked.

"I'm not sure," he muttered. "It's just a very weird scenario. I didn't really expect it to be as uncomfortable as it is, and yet, in a way, I should have, I guess. But … that's just the way it is."

She laughed. "When you're gone for a while, and you

come back, you know there will always be a certain level of awkwardness."

"Maybe, and I didn't expect to come back, but neither did I expect to find that they blamed her quite so much. Apparently I was expected to take over the ranch at some point, and, when I left, Jake felt that very keenly."

"Maybe that's when the stepson got all this nonsense in his head. You know, as in higher expectations and getting a bigger piece of the pie."

"And that's possible, though I don't know that we'll ever know the answer to that one," Austin admitted. "I just know that, right now, things are pretty dysfunctional."

"That's just the norm for families," Kat cut in. "Some work through it, and some don't, so don't put yourself into the hot seat over that one."

He snorted. "Considering that a lot of the problems here started right after I left, it's hard not to."

"Again, you have to look after yourself," Kat stated. "I didn't send you there to decimate your own soul. You need to work through this so you can come back healthy and happy." There was silence while he contemplated that. She jumped into the silence. "Are you okay?"

"Yes, … I am. It's just a very strange scenario."

"Not really. You were fine without her all these years, so just finish up your job, do what you think you need to do in terms of who took the dog, since we don't want that scenario to happen again, then come home." And, with that, she spoke a moment more and hung up.

Austin sat here on the bed for a long moment, contemplating Kat's words. As soon as he thought about *going home*, everything inside of him revolted. He looked around the room, realizing that, although this wasn't the room he had used when he was married to Rox, it was still very much part of the place that he'd carried in his own mind, even now considering it *home*.

And that was the problem because, as long as he left his relationship with Rox unresolved, he wouldn't find any peace. He needed to get to that point, first and foremost, before he could walk away. But the real question hounding him was if he was prepared to walk away again.

CHAPTER 10

R OX GOT UP super early the next morning after a bad night, then wandered the house in the early morning half-shadow, half-light conditions, holding a cup of coffee in her hand as she contemplated the changes in her own life circumstances. Leaving the ranch had never been an option for her. It had always been about continuity, keeping the family line in ownership, keeping everything that the generations before her had worked so hard to maintain. Yet, for the first time, she wondered about the sacrifices every generation had made in order to keep together the dream of other people, people who were long gone.

She knew it would be a horrible shame to have this beautiful ranch broken up or sold as is to some commercial entity, and yet that's what was happening all around them. It was also partly why her father was so adamant to ensure that they kept their land, and she understood that. She really did. But, at some point in time, she wasn't sure that she could keep up with what she thought needed to be kept up.

They had money issues. They had equipment failures. They had staffing issues, and, more than anything else, it was a lonely life. She'd already cornered the market on loneliness as far she was concerned, and maybe it was time to knock it free. Hearing a noise behind her, she turned, expecting to see her mom, but instead it was Austin, standing there, his crossed arms, looking at her. She frowned at him.

He smiled. "I love how some mannerisms never change."

"Such as?" she asked in a clipped tone.

"The minute you see me, when you weren't expecting to see me, you frown as if it's the worst thing in the world."

"It certainly isn't the *worst* thing in my world," she corrected, staring at him. "It's just an instinctive reaction."

"Sure, it is, and it's also one that gives me the weirdest feeling. That, *oh it's you*, instead of *oh, it's you*," he clarified, with the smallest tentative grin.

She flushed, feeling the heat rise up and down her cheeks at his comment. "I think the time for that is long past, isn't it?"

"I don't know," he replied, taking the last step toward her. "I guess we have to decide whether anything is left between us."

She looked at him in astonishment. "You didn't come home for five years, Austin," she pointed out. "So, I'm pretty sure nothing is between us."

"Yeah, but you didn't ask me to come home either. So I took it as a sign that you didn't want me to. What if we were both wrong?"

She shook her head, not even sure what to do with this version of the man she thought she'd known so well. Yet obviously she didn't. After he had walked away, she hadn't been able to forget about him. "I was young and stupid, … but I'm not anymore."

"Good," he noted. "There was room for growing up, and there was also room for me to change. I think that's what life is all about. You make a choice, a decision. You live with it, and you move on and hope that you make a better one the next time."

She stared at him, her jaw working, and finally the question that she desperately needed answered burst out. "Do you regret leaving?"

He looked at her and smiled. "I guess that's one of the questions we should address, isn't it?"

"And that was an evasive maneuver," she declared, with a wave of her hand.

"You got the question out before I did," he said, with a smile. "Did you regret my leaving?" When she didn't answer right away, he dove in. "I don't know that you did, but maybe it was necessary for both of us to experience that. Maybe we were both young and stupid. I don't know," he said. "I look back on it and wonder if I would have done something differently. I couldn't *not* go since I was already committed to the military, but should I have come back and talked to you about it? Maybe. Did you piss me off by putting me in that position? Yeah, you sure did. But did I need to be that pissed off? Probably not," he admitted. "At some point in time it was too much, so coming back didn't seem to be much of an option."

"So, you just kept running," she whispered.

"Maybe. I took on one mission after another that kept me away. So the longer I was gone, the harder it was to change course," he shared.

She nodded, and she felt something inside her sighing ever-so-slightly. "I can get behind that," she murmured, "because I felt the same way."

"That's the thing. We both backed ourselves into a corner, didn't we?" he asked, with a wry smile. "Then there was no moving forward. It was what it was, and we were just stuck there. You probably would have changed it, if you had the time, but you didn't have time. You didn't have the opportunity, and you didn't create it because you thought it was already water under the bridge. Thus, you found a way to adapt and to move on."

"Until you show up out of the blue and realize that adapting and moving on didn't let you move on at all."

He laughed. "That's the trick, isn't it? Adapting and moving on is one thing, but moving on without having dealt with everything else is a completely different thing."

She nodded. "So, what I need to know," she began, "is anything still between us, or did you literally just come here for Cowboy?"

"Cowboy was certainly one of the reasons, and Kat pushing me to come and deal with my history was another," he replied, with a wry smile. "She's a very smart woman."

"Your prosthetic designer, right?"

He nodded. "Badger and I served in the military together years ago. We've always kept in touch, and he's kind of a hub for a lot of lost dogs," he quipped, with half a sigh. "A lot of lost soldiers too."

"Is that what you are right now?"

"No," he declared, a smile on his face. "Was I ever? I don't know. Probably. It's hard, after a life-changing injury, to know what you're supposed to do with your life anymore—or how you're supposed to do it—because you don't have the same abilities anymore. That's probably why I would never contemplate coming back here because … I'm just not the man I used to be. I'm not physically the man I used to be, and I can't do the work I used to do. And I know that one of the things most wanted here, most needed here, and most valued here is physical strength and capability," he conceded. "At this point in my life, I don't have the same strength, ability, and fitness level I did before. I probably can't even keep up with Jake."

"Yet I don't think he would agree with that."

"No, he probably wouldn't, but I've never asked him, and I won't."

"Pride?" she asked.

"I don't know if it's pride," he replied, "but it's very humbling to have an injury that requires you to stop and reassess your world. If nothing else during rehab, I took a close look at the decisions I made and wondered if they were the right ones, but I have to believe they were the right ones at the time. We can tear ourselves apart with *what ifs*," he noted, as he shook his head and looked out to the yard, "but the real trick is sorting out what to do now, as you sit here and contemplate something different."

She stepped back, so he could have better access to the counter, and muttered, "There's coffee."

"I assumed there was, since you're hanging on to that cup with a death grip," he teased, as his lips twitched. "That is something else you used to do a lot of."

She stared at him. "What are you talking about?"

"When you were upset or didn't like something, the cup was almost a prop for you, and you hung on to it just as you are now, as if you'll try to get through this the best you can, and then you'll break down afterward. I'm not here to make you break down. I'm just here to find peace, so I can go on somehow."

"Peace so you can go on without me, right?"

He stopped, studied her, and from the look on his face she figured he'd seen the regret on her face. But maybe not...

She nodded, turned on her heel, and headed out onto the deck. It was all she could do to hold back the tears, to hold back everything, and to make it through this next little bit. She hoped he would just get some coffee and would leave her alone, leave her alone with the world she had created for herself.

As she stared out at the big, wide world around her, she realized it really was time. It was time to stop hanging on to hope, time to stop hanging on to anything connected to Austin, thinking he would come back one day and would be the person she thought he was and had always hoped he would come back to being.

As she stood there and bowed her head, strong arms reached around her shoulders, and she was tugged gently against a chest. She knew it was him, but she hadn't expected this compassion or even this gentleness. She didn't know what the hell she had expected, but it wasn't this.

He held her close and whispered, "I don't know that what we had is something that we want to continue ... because what we had was young, painful, immature, and not very comfortable for either one of us. If either of us had thought otherwise, I would have returned, and you would have called me. Yet what we could have now could be better."

She slowly turned in his arms and looked at him in astonishment.

He shrugged. "Obviously you haven't moved on, and neither have I. ... I don't even know if you're interested in trying again, but, when I first got here, it was an absolute *hell no*." His lips twitched. "But an apparently absolute *hell, no* doesn't really apply once we start to really see each other again."

"I never wanted to hurt you, you know?" she murmured.

"No, you might not have wanted to, not deep down," he

conceded, "but, in that moment, that's exactly what you wanted to do. I just don't know why, and, because I couldn't figure out what I had done—and I was tired of all that pettiness—I just moved on."

"You moved on?" she asked, frowning.

"No. I didn't move on in that way," he conceded, with half a laugh. He tucked her back into his arms.

Rox went willingly, resting her head against his chest, wondering with a sense of awe if there was actually any hope for them.

Austin added, "I'm not saying that I want to go back to what we had." She immediately stiffened, tried to pull back, but he held her close and continued. "Because what we had didn't last, and, if we try again, I want to ensure it's something that comes from honesty and openness, something that would withstand the test of time. It's been very lonely without you, but it was also my fault, and I accept responsibility for that."

She looked up, feeling the tears in her eyes. "That was also *classic you*. If ever anybody needed to apologize, you stepped up and did it first," she muttered. "Sometimes I hated you for that." When he looked at her in astonishment, she grinned. "Because it always made me feel as if I was *less than*."

"Good God, Rox," Austin muttered. "I just always tried to step up and to be the person who I wanted to be. And sometimes it was easier for me to do than others," he noted, "but it was never *ever* to make you look or feel bad."

"I know that now," she shared, "and, as I've realized over these last few years, it really had nothing to do with you and everything to do with me. I just wasn't ready to grow up, to be mature, and to accept responsibility for my own actions. ... For all of that, I'm sorry."

"Me too," he said, "but I'm also sorry for my own actions."

And, with that, she rested against his chest, wondering at the joy and the sense of homecoming of having his arms wrapped around her.

"So, is that a yes?" he asked.

"A yes to what?" she asked, looking back at him, her eyes narrowing. "I think we need to be very clear about what it is we're looking for this time."

"A yes to seeing if anything is here that we want to work on," he replied. "A yes to going back and trying this again. A yes to your not sending me away when you're pissed off."

She winced. "And how about a yes to your not leaving, in case I lose my temper and push you away?" She took a deep breath to add, "And understand that, if I do try to push you away, it's because I'm hurting, hurting so bad that it's an instinctive reaction to be alone. And that it's not about you. It's all about me, trying to protect myself somehow."

"So, maybe you just need to tell me what hurt you so badly that you needed to kick me away."

"You guys had just come back in from being outside, you and Dad. I don't even know what you were working on, but you were laughing and joking, and Dad, ... he slapped an arm around your shoulders, called you *son*, as if he was so proud of you. It was just one of those moments when I realized that, no matter what I did, no matter what I wanted to do, no matter how hard I worked or how much I achieved, I would never be what Dad really wanted me to be. His *son*."

Austin winced, reality dawning. "So, I somehow became the object of that anger?"

"No, it wasn't that you were the object of my anger, but you were the one I could kick at safely and know that you wouldn't retaliate. I could vent as much and as hard as I wanted to and could let go of all that pain and all that torment of a lifetime trying to achieve, trying to be something that Dad would be proud of. But instead of being that person I thought I could trust, who would always be there for me, the one place it was safe to be honest, you took my words, you took my pain, and, instead of helping me work through it, you walked away, and that was something I found incredibly difficult to forgive."

He stared at her for a long moment. "Wow. … I never once even thought that you would be so jealous of my relationship with your father that it would impact your relationship with him—or with me. I thought getting along with your parents was a plus in our marriage. Maybe you were seeing things that weren't there, not seeing what was right in front of you. Rox, you are the apple of Jake's eye and always have been."

"I may be the apple of his eye, but I'm still a female," she clarified, trying hard to keep out the bitterness, "and in that way I can never be what he wanted."

"And neither should you try," Austin pointed out. "You are better than what he wanted in that sense. He may not know it, and he might not have any idea that you feel that way, but the bottom line is that he absolutely adores you just the way you are," Austin said. "It never once occurred to me that you were lashing out at me as a safe place to put your pain. I had no idea and took every bit of it to heart."

"I wasn't thinking clearly."

He shrugged. "You're right though. When you do love somebody, you do need a safe space," he stated, "and hopefully at some point in time there won't be that level of anger. I feel so foolish now that I didn't stick around long enough to see it dissipate."

She winced. "I'm not saying this is all about you and what you did wrong," she pointed out. "I've done an awful lot of work on myself, and I know there is still an awful lot to be done, but thankfully I do feel as if I'm a whole lot better off now than I was before."

He nodded, his arms tightening gently around her, hugging her close. "You are, and in many ways I am too, but still, it's a bit of a shock to hear your side of it."

"Which, if you had come home that day …"

He smiled and nodded. "I might have heard that," he noted, "or I might not have because you might not have been at a point where you could tell me that yet."

She nodded. "I'm not sure I was back then," she admitted. "One of the hardest things to realize is just how much I've grown and how much I could have done back then to put a stop to it, as it all seems so foolish now."

"And yet, five years later, here we are," he said, with a chuckle.

"Five years," she muttered, as she stared out at the world. "How the hell did five years go by so fast?"

"It went by in the blink of an eye, and the next five will too," he noted, "unless we want to do something about it. If we'll go for it, we need to make these next five years count for something between us."

"You're right. We can't go back to what we had," she agreed, and he stiffened ever-so-slightly. She looked up at him and added, "We need to ensure our time together is one full of trust, not just lust."

"Oh, there was plenty of that," he chuckled, giving her a

bright smile, "and, in my experience, it's a great thing, but we also knew we loved each other too. Maybe somewhere along the line we got lost somehow, but …"

"I don't even know whether we lost that love," she clarified, "or it just got buried under our own insecurities."

"That was also when Chris was causing trouble, wasn't it?"

She nodded. "Yeah, though I don't know how much trouble it actually was because, I wasn't included in those conversations, especially after you left. If you'd been here, I would have been included," she said, without rancor.

"You think so?"

She nodded. "Yes, I think so. … I know so. Dad was very much starting to treat me like my mother, you know, *keeping all the dangerous things away from the womenfolk.*"

"Right," he agreed, with a smile. "That's pretty instinctive too, from a male point of view."

"Maybe," she muttered, "but it's also pretty irritating."

He burst out laughing and nodded. "I can see that, so I will try to include you in more than just the decisions that your father would think you should be aware of," he promised, with a smile. "I'm also very big these days on making sure that women know how to protect themselves. Unfortunately I've seen way too much ugliness in the world. Even without that, I want to protect you and to keep you safe and to know you can help yourself as well."

She cuddled even closer. "That would be nice," she murmured, "but I still feel as if we have a long way to go before we get anything settled."

"I don't even know that there is such a thing," he said, as he massaged her back. "We just have to ensure that we're a whole lot closer and more open to communication than we ever have been before because, although we thought we had something great between us, it fell apart when it was really tested."

"Right," she agreed, "and now I'm not allowed to send you away."

"No, you're not," he confirmed. "I don't think I ever told you, but that was the thing that my father did to us—and then my mother also."

She turned to frown at him. "But your family is together."

"Now, yes, but back then, no. They were at each other's throats more often than not. My father kicked us out of the house, saying he was done being a father and didn't want anything to do with the entire mess. There'd been ... I don't know, some cacophony at home. Anyway he made it very clear, and I don't remember how old I was, but I do remember my mom packing us up and all of us leaving. It went back and forth for quite a while, but I was pretty devastated, and now when ultimatums are given? ... I just remember Mom packing up and moving us, and me automatically doing the same, as an adult. Anyway, she remarried a while back and lives overseas now."

She nodded in understanding.

He looked down at her. "Because if there's one thing you do when you're hurting ..."

Hearing him say it, she knew what he was feeling and completed his sentence. "You run away and hide."

"Exactly, and that's not just a female trait," he stated. *"You don't want me? Fine, I don't want you either, and I'm gone."*

"So, I will try my hardest not to send you away."

"And I will try not to react in the same way," he added, a

smile on his face, "and we will communicate better from now on."

She smiled. "Yes."

He hesitated and whispered, "I was gone a long time."

"Yes, you were."

"Was there anybody else? Will I have to face neighbors in town who know of some … old boyfriends?"

She shook her head. "No. None. You were gone five years, and, in that time, I didn't date. I didn't do anything. I was pretty upset and angry for a long time, and then I just became very sad," she shared. "My parents tried hard to send me back out to the world, not dating, just joining some people in a book club or whatever, but I just wasn't interest-ed."

He held her close and nodded.

"What about you?" she asked. "You always had oppor-tunities at every corner of the world."

"There are always opportunities," he conceded, with a nod, "but that doesn't mean those were choices I made."

Hearing a sound behind them, he stepped back and sug-gested, "I think we should keep this to ourselves for a little bit." She looked up at him in surprise, and he shrugged. "We still aren't 100 percent sure on where we're at or how we'll handle jumping in. At the moment, it's private and just between us. You know what would happen once your parents find out."

She winced and nodded. "I would appreciate that too," she agreed. "Before, it seemed as if everything about our relationship was completely open, and everybody knew everything. It made things really difficult when you left because I didn't have anything to say. I didn't know what to say."

"You don't have to say anything," he declared. "That's the thing. You don't have to say anything because it is still your life. Your business is just that … *yours*."

"But when you live and work on a family ranch like this," Rox pointed out, "it's like living in a fish bowl."

"So, let's change that. Let's work on us first," he suggested.

She pointed at the kitchen. "Come on. You never did get coffee, did you?"

"No, I didn't."

As he stepped inside, he felt something so terribly wrong, and his instincts were screaming at him. Cowboy was standing at his side, and his left hand automatically went to the dog's shoulder, as his right hand when to Rox's. Then he heard that telltale sound. He grabbed Rox and pulled her to the floor, just as multiple shots were fired, and the space above their heads splintered,

Then everything went completely silent.

CHAPTER 11

"**O**H MY GOD, oh my God," Rox whispered, still on the floor with Cowboy and Austin. "Somebody's shooting at us."

Austin nodded, his face grim, as he shimmied over to the window, stared out just a hair to the side, trying to see outside without being caught. "I don't know if they're still there. Do you know who's at the bunkhouse?"

She nodded. "Both Carlos and Raul will be over there, and, other than Raul's one and only handgun, they're both defenseless."

"Send them a message and tell them to stay where they are."

At that came the sound of Jake thundering down the stairs. The big man was never light on his feet, but, when it came time to rush, he was a bull in a china shop. As he raced toward them, Austin tackled him before he burst out the door. "Calm down, big man, calm down."

"What do you mean, *calm down?*" he snarled, as he looked at him. "Somebody out there is shooting at the house," Jake yelled.

Austin nodded. "We just barely saved our own heads, and I don't want you going out there and taking a direct hit."

At that, Jake stared at him, calming down ever-so-slightly, and looking over them both. "Are you two okay?"

"Yes, we're both fine," Austin replied, "but whoever the hell is outside is not playing. Those were head shots," he snapped. "Did you let the FBI take all those guns out of here?"

"Sure, I did," he muttered. "Not as if you can argue with the FBI. Just remember that you didn't want those guns here, thinking the gun-runners would come here after them, but look at what's happening now.

"They probably are here looking for them, and now we don't have them to give back."

"As if you would give them back anyway," Austin scoffed.

Jake shrugged half-heartedly. "Of course I wouldn't."

"I'm not sure that they're necessarily here after the guns as much as giving us a warning, a deadly one," he added thoughtfully, as he looked outside again. "Although maybe they have more stashes on your land." With that said, Austin frowned and faced Jake.

"Those weren't warning shots," Rox declared, staring at them. "No way in hell. It was just way too directed."

"It was, wasn't it?" Austin murmured, as he considered that. "Still, they must have known that, if their cache was found, no way they would get it back."

"So, what the hell are they pissed off about?" Jake asked.

"They're pissed off that they got caught," she stated.

Austin grinned and nodded. "Exactly, and that means they didn't think they would get caught."

"Why not?" Jake asked.

"Because they have somebody on the inside," Rox suggested slowly. "That's what you meant, isn't it, Austin?"

"Yeah, that's my take on it," Austin murmured, "and I

know it's not what either one of you want to contemplate."

"Of course not," Rox snapped. "Very few of us are here, as you know, and we can only blame a couple, before we have to look at the rest of us."

At that, with no further sound of gunfire, their phones were heating up from calls and texts sent from the men in the bunkhouse.

Jake read one of his texts. "Raul saw a vehicle take off down the highway."

Austin asked, "Can he describe the vehicle? Did he get a license plate? Did he see who got into it?"

Jake called him instead of texting, and Raul's tone was excited, as he tried to pass on the information. Jake passed it along. "Somebody ran through the yard shooting, then kept on going right to the highway and got in the vehicle and took off."

"That's the good news," Austin noted. "The bad news is that we don't know who it was, unless Raul can identify him."

Jake shook his head. "All he saw was someone wearing a long trench coat, the kind that we wear when we're out riding, plus a hat, a cowboy hat."

"Of course it was a cowboy hat," Austin muttered. "That with a duster makes for damn good coverage."

"It might be damn good coverage," Jake noted, "but somebody should have seen him."

"Do you have security? Cameras or anything?"

"No, we don't have security around the ranch. You know that."

"I do know that," Austin muttered. "It's one of the things we used to argue about all the time."

Jake snorted. "Would have been a lot of money spent

over the years if I had put it in."

"And right now we would also have an idea of who the hell was in the yard shooting at us," Austin snapped right back. He'd never been one to let Jake tromp on him, but Jake was a tough man to be around, and this was another prime example.

"If it happens again, maybe we'll look at it," Jake said grudgingly.

"And if it happens again, you may not have a choice."

"Meaning that I would have to?"

"No, meaning that you won't be here to make the choice," Austin declared. "I get that, for you, it's all about honor and being good neighbors and being a moral person and all that, and I'm right there with you on all that. However, I spent way too much time in wars and gunfights and strife, seeing the bowels of humanity, seeing the danger of minimizing the seriousness of what's going on here right now."

"You really think somebody is after us?" Jake asked.

"Don't you?" Austin asked in a challenging voice. "Just think about what you've said right now. You're thinking that it's the guys who had the weapons cache, and that would make sense, but you're also thinking that they're just here after their weapons. That they're not here as a threat, that they're not out here for anything else," Austin spelled out, "but I can't see that because there was no need for them to come here."

Rox added, "Unless they were trying to keep us pinned here while they did something else."

"Exactly," Austin agreed. "So you guys stay here. I'm heading back out to where that cache of weapons was."

"The hell you are," Jake roared. "This is still my place,

God damn it."

"Then get off your ass and let's go," Austin snapped, not breaking stride as he flung open the front door and raced to the barn, quickly saddling up Charlie.

Jake suggested, "You could take a four-wheeler."

"You can," Austin replied, "or take the truck down the highway. I'll go in through the back to see if I can find them while they're busy racing away, thinking they're off the hook."

With that, they split up.

Austin took Charlie through the back way, as Jake headed to the truck. It would have been faster to go his direction for sure, but Austin was not at all certain that every one of the shooters would be heading out the same way. So if the shooters split up, Austin wanted to know who was taking part in what.

With that, he put Charlie into a flat-out gallop, as they raced toward the next confrontation.

CHAPTER 12

ROX RACED WITH her father to the truck, as he roared at her, "Get back in the house."

"No," she snapped, "I'm not going back. I'm coming to help figure out what the hell is going on here. You want me to look after this place? I need to know just what you're signing me up for."

"It sure as hell wasn't supposed to be this crap," he cried out, as they both climbed inside the truck, Cowboy jumping into the back seat, and he shifted it into gear and pulled back out and raced down the long driveway. He kept to one of the side roads, heading back to where the cache of weapons had been found.

"Do you really think it's Chris?" she asked him.

"I sure as hell hope not. That'll break your mama's heart."

"I think it's already broken," Rox noted. "I don't know what happened between the two of you the last time Chris acted out, but Mom hasn't been quite the same since."

He shot her a hard look and snapped, "And I ain't talking."

"You might not be talking, but you're also not helping things by *not* talking."

"What the hell?" he muttered. "Is nobody listening to me anymore?"

"We listen, and then we make decisions on our own. Right now, whatever is going on with you and Mom is a problem."

"That is because you're living too close."

"Maybe," she replied, "but, unless you're kicking me off the ranch, I am staying right here."

"I won't kick you off the place," he muttered. "Don't be ridiculous, but you also can't stick your nose into what's not your business."

"Depends whether it's not my business or *should* become my business," she clarified. "I don't know what's going on at this ranch. I really hope it's all minor, but it doesn't feel minor at all."

"Of course it doesn't feel minor," he snapped. "Divorces are never minor."

She stopped, her breath catching in the back of her throat. "You and Mom?"

"Maybe," he conceded. "We're definitely struggling. I don't want to see it come to that, and I sure as hell hope we can get past it, but, at the moment, things are a little dicey."

"Jesus Christ." She moaned, as she sagged into the passenger seat.

"Yeah, so you feel better now for knowing?"

"Maybe, maybe not," she muttered. "Been there, done that."

"It didn't work out so well for you, did it?"

"Maybe not, but maybe it will now."

He turned, giving her a sharp look. "Are you guys making up?"

"Let's just say that we're talking."

"That would be a godsend if you did," he muttered. "I have to admit it's been pretty stressful since you guys split."

"Maybe," she agreed, "but that was my problem, not yours. Your problem was to keep Mom happy."

"Sure, and how am I supposed to do that when her son has been stealing from me every time I turn around?" When Rox turned to stare at him in shock, he nodded. "You want to handle this place when I'm gone, then you've got to handle that brother of yours."

"What the hell is his problem?" she asked.

"You already know his problem. He wants the property."

"But he never did before all this. I don't remember his ever caring."

"That doesn't mean that he didn't care. I think he was just biding his time, but finding out the truth was a whole different story."

"Finding out what truth? Chris was decent up until Austin left, and then things just fell apart."

"As did everything else around here," Jake growled. "We're going up here," he said, pointing out the road. As they got closer and took another turn off the highway, she hung on for dear life as he blasted through to the area where the weapons had been found.

"Did you bring a weapon with you?" she asked.

He snorted. "I brought two."

"Good," she muttered. "I've just got my handgun."

"Be prepared to use it," Jake spat. "Things could get ugly, and, if you die, God help you."

"Why is that?" she asked, amusement in her tone.

"Because I'll have to go back into hell to find you and to drag your sorry ass out. Your mama will kill me if I don't bring you home in one piece."

She smiled at him. "Ah, Dad, I know you love me."

He gave her a sharp look. "What the hell? What is wrong

with everybody around here?" He shook his head, "Of course I love you. Nothing will ever change that."

"No," she muttered, her tone light and more serene than she could have expected, "but, every once in a while, we forget it and need to be reminded."

He just shook his head, as he hit the brakes, pulling off to the side. Then he grabbed his rifle and barked, "Let's go."

The two of them were out of the truck and running toward where the cache had been. She'd barely even gotten a look before because it had been nighttime, so getting out here right now in daylight was interesting. There wasn't a soul around as far as she could see. At the same time, not a single bird sang. Absolutely nothing could be heard except the silence of an early morning. She and Jake stilled, taking a quieter approach now. She muttered, "It's too quiet."

"It absolutely is too quiet," Jake confirmed. "I don't like anything about it."

A hushed whistle came from one side, and she frowned as she turned to look in that direction. "That sounds like Austin."

Jake raised one eyebrow at her. "At least you know his whistles."

"I do, and I also know that one was a warning." She pulled her father quietly off to the side. "He's seeing something we aren't."

"Maybe, but we can't just stay here and hide," Jake stated. "That just isn't my style."

"No, but my style isn't getting my ass shot up either," Rox added, "so a little bit of caution would be good."

"Yeah, well, caution is one thing," Jake noted, "and being foolhardy is stupid, so get down."

As she ducked down, he stepped out and roared, "What

the hell do you want with my land and my family?"

When the bullet came, it picked him up off his feet and flattened him to the ground. Instantly gunfire lit the air, and chaos was all around.

She raced over to her father's side. The bullet was probably intended for his head, but nobody quite understood the size of the man, and he took it in the shoulder. As he stared up at her in shock, she whispered, "Get over to the truck. You're shot in the shoulder, nowhere else, so let's ensure it stays that way."

But he was already stumbling to his feet, swearing a blue streak.

"I'll go help Austin," she said, trying to calm down her father.

"I'm coming too," he roared, as he got into place, tucked in behind her.

The fact that he would even let her take the lead was something else, but it also confirmed that he was hurt just enough to realize he needed help.

As they came up to a hollow, she heard voices, and sure enough one was Austin, calm as ever. Yet, as she peered around the bush, she saw him standing there, his hands over his head, a weapon held against him. She didn't recognize the other man at all.

"What the hell are you doing here?" the stranger asked Austin.

"We heard a racket and headed out here, particularly after yesterday's find," Austin replied. "We figured there might be more."

"You should have just stayed inside. We came to get the rest of our stuff before you decided to get nosy and to steal more of it."

"We didn't steal anything," Austin stated casually. "You and I both know Texas law, and, if it's on our property, we get to keep it."

"It wouldn't have been so bad if you just kept it, but you didn't, did you? You brought in the cops."

Austin laughed. "What do you expect? I don't even know who the hell you are."

"So, it really doesn't matter to me one bit. I can pop a stranger just as well as I can pop a friend."

"And that takes a special talent," Austin noted. "Somebody who just doesn't give a shit for either side. You're not here alone, so these guys you're paying to be with you, do they know that you would throw them to the wolves just as easily?"

"I don't think they give a shit. As long as they get their money, I would say they're good."

"Right, it's all about mercenaries. How many caches do you have out here?"

"Not telling you about them on the slim chance that you get out of this," he replied. "The last thing I need is for you to be coming back after us."

"I can tell you without a doubt that you can count on Jake coming after you."

"Not likely. I already popped him one," he said, with a snort. "He's not going anywhere. And that'll make somebody out there very happy."

"You mean Chris? I don't think he would go that far," Austin declared, shaking his head. "He might be a confused and disturbed man, but I don't think killing his family was part of his plan."

"Well then, you don't really know him, do you?" The man cackled with reckless laughter. "Because believe me that he wanted his father, his stepfather," he corrected, "to not see the light of day again."

"Interesting. I wouldn't have thought Chris was that angry."

"You really don't know him then, do you? Now turn around and walk."

"And if I don't?"

"I'll shoot you right here then."

"So, what's the difference?" Austin asked. "I would much rather face my killer than have a bullet in the back. That's the coward's way."

"Are you calling me a coward?"

"Sure, I am," he confirmed, with a snort. "If you're planning on shooting me in the back, I can call you anything I want."

"I didn't say I would shoot you at all," he stated, "but, if that's what you want, I'm all for it."

"No, you aren't," Austin argued.

She couldn't believe that Austin was antagonizing the shooter, and she wasn't at all sure that she could get close enough to do anything, and then she saw Cowboy coming up through the brush, Charlie standing there too. Charlie nickered and walked forward ever-so-slightly, and she wanted to call out to him and tell him to stop.

The gunman looked over at the horse and nodded. "Interesting choice of horses."

"One of the old guys. Charlie's always been good to me," Austin stated. "I don't have a problem bringing him out when he wants to go for a run."

"It's not that he wants to go for a run," he argued. "God, that's such a typical cowboy attitude."

"Really? You think he doesn't like to be out here? It's not

as if I'm working him hard," Austin said, with half a smile, "and I don't think Charlie and I got a problem at all. But you might be the kind of person who always thinks you've got a problem."

"People got problems. They've always got problems. They just don't recognize what those problems are," the stranger declared. "But right now I've got to get the hell out of here, and I want to get the rest of my caches, so I need you to just disappear. Seeing how you won't, I'll have to make you." As he raised the gun to fire, Cowboy jumped up from behind and snapped down hard on his wrist, bringing the man and his weapon to the ground.

As the gunman swore and cursed, trying to fight off the dog, Rox raced forward with her own gun out, just in time to watch Austin do some flip kick and drop the man flat to the ground, holding him there almost effortlessly.

"I don't think you'll be doing anything," Austin snapped, "because I don't have any intention of letting you go." Austin didn't need to do anything else, since Cowboy's teeth were still attached to the gunman's arm.

"What the fuck?" the gunman roared. "Don't you understand? I need to get those caches."

"You should have thought about that before you shot Jake and tried to shoot me," Austin snapped.

Rox watched in shock as Austin revved back his right hand and plowed it into the gunman's jawbone, rendering the man suddenly relaxed and completely limp. She raced over. "Oh my God, are you okay?"

"I'm fine," he said, giving her a big smile.

AUSTIN SMILED UP at Rox, and, with her help, straightened up and gave her a big hug. "How's your dad?"

"I'm fine," snapped Jake, as he leaned against a nearby tree. "What the hell is going on here?"

"Apparently more caches of weapons are scattered around the property. He was here to clear out some more before we found them."

"You mentioned how you thought there would be more."

Austin shrugged. "It didn't make any sense that there wouldn't be more. If it was me, I wouldn't hide them all in one place either."

At that, Jake snorted. "That makes sense too," he muttered. "What the hell?" He stared at the unconscious gunman. "Who is this? … He is kind of familiar looking."

Rox nodded. "I thought so too. Still can't place him."

Austin frowned, taking note. "Jake, you need to get law enforcement in here to pick him up."

Jake groaned at that. "The sheriff is already pissed off at me because I cut him out of the action to begin with."

"Well, this one is his, so give him a shout, and then we'll see from the sheriff's reaction when he actually gets here if he knows our gunman."

"Do you really think he does?" Rox asked.

"I don't know whether he does or not," Austin admitted. "I'm hoping he doesn't, but somebody local knows where this stuff is hidden. We also need to keep Cowboy out here, tracking any firearms that he can. He was trained in that, per my boss, so we should use him."

"You really think Cowboy can do that?" Jake asked.

"He already has. Remember that he's the one who kept bugging me and Rox to follow him, and this is where he led us." He looked over at Rox. "You okay?"

She looked up at him and smiled. She walked over, and, instead of giving him a hug or a kiss, she punched him in the gut.

He stared at her in surprise. "What was that for?"

"That's for telling me that line of shit about not being physically fit, not being the same man, not being in the peak condition you used to be in, and that your injuries made a difference."

He shrugged. "It does make a hell of a difference."

"*Yeah, right,*" she scoffed. "And yet who's on the ground now?"

"An asshole who will stay there," Austin spat out. With that, he pulled her into his arms and gave her a big kiss. She laughed as she stepped back and looked over at her father, who was staring at the two of them.

Then a sparkle came in his eyes, and he nodded. "Damn high time," he muttered. "Your mama and I'd just about lost hope."

"Don't count on anything right now," Austin stated. "Just because we're looking at trying again, we sure as hell don't need or want any interference or pressure from you guys. It'll be a while, as we sort through some issues."

"You take all the time you want," Jake stated, with a big grin. Then the grin fell away from his face. "We need to get this asshole out of here and find those other weapons."

"We need to do it fast too," Austin said, nodding in agreement. "The last time I saw this guy, he had two cohorts with him. Not exactly the kind of guys we would necessarily want to keep around, so whether they're coming back, looking for the other weapons, or looking for this guy, we'll have more trouble than we expect."

"I just sent his photo to Raul. This guy is not the one who was shooting up the house," Rox shared, "so we have to keep that in mind too."

"Right, so there are at least two others, possibly a third, but I'm betting that one of those other two was the one shooting at the house," Austin suggested. "I didn't get a look at them because I was still hunkered down on the floor. So I have no idea on gait or height or anything, but this guy could certainly have been at the house with his other buddies. Then they split up and took different ways out of there."

At that, he looked over at Rox and said, "Get your father back to the ranch, so he can get his shoulder looked at. He'll have to go to the medical clinic, and I really don't want to hear any argument," he declared, turning to look at the big man. "I know you don't want to leave, but, in this case, you have to."

Jake grimaced. "I'm in just enough pain that I won't argue with you," he muttered. "She sure as hell better drive carefully on the way back. Otherwise it'll hurt like shit."

"It'll hurt like shit anyway," she said, as she walked toward him. "Nothing I can do about that. You don't get to blame me for my driving on fields and country roads because you got yourself shot up."

"Not blaming you," he protested, but still growling. The two of them wrangled over in the direction of the vehicle. Then she stopped, looked back at Austin, and asked, "What are you doing?"

"Standing guard," he replied. "Cowboy and I will stay here, and Charlie will stay too."

With that said, almost as if both animals understood, they moved closer to Austin.

Rox nodded and smiled. "You've got Dad's rifle?"

"I've got your father's rifle," he stated, with a nod. "Now go get him taken care of."

"I don't want to leave until we have law enforcement here," Jake said, turning and glaring at him.

Rox agreed. "We'll stay until somebody comes here to help as backup."

"That's fine," Austin relented, "as long as you get the hell out of here and look after yourself as soon as they arrive."

Jake just glared at him and finally nodded. "Fine," he muttered, and then he grinned. "Glad to have you back. I'll go sit in the goddamn truck." And Jake slowly made his way over to the big truck he'd come in on.

Rox looked back at Austin, who just smiled and nodded. "It's fine. I'll be fine right here."

"*Sure*," she quipped, "but you're the one who was just saying that other men are likely coming."

"Yeah, they sure are," he agreed, waving his hands. "I'm already looking to set up a plan of some sort. It'll be a whole lot better if I don't have to worry about you two as well." She glared at him, and he nodded. "I know. You don't like it, but that is just the way it needs to be in this case. Jake is hurt, and, as much I know he would like to come, guns ablazing, come hell or high water, but that shoulder is already paining him."

"I'm not so weak that I can't stand a little bit of pain either," Jake roared from the distance.

Rox laughed. "It would be nice if, just one time, Dad would, ... you know, calm down a little bit."

"And then you wouldn't even know who he is," Austin murmured. "I'll be fine. You go with him. I've got a weapon.

I've got the dog and a horse."

"Sure," she said, "but you don't have backup, and Dad won't leave until you've got that."

"Fine," Austin muttered. "At least be stationed so you can keep an eye on him *and* the road."

"Right," she replied, "but I still don't like leaving you here."

"I get it, but law enforcement should be here soon enough."

"How do you know one of the other assholes isn't out here looking for this gunman already?"

"I'm counting on it," Austin declared, with half a smile. "I doubt they will all be here though. I suspect we'll have to roust one or two of them out from the hollows or wherever they're hiding." Her eyebrows shot up at that, and he nodded. "Not today's worry."

"That will hardly make me feel better."

"No, it won't, but remember that this is what I do. They're in my world, as much as I'm in theirs."

"*Right.* I'm not sure I want to think about that very much either," she noted.

He smiled. "We can always talk when I get back."

"We'll also have to talk to Mom and Dad because they'll be all over us this time."

"Maybe, but we need to take it slow, and we need to ensure it's our decision, not theirs. We already know how they feel about it, but that won't be helpful in the long run."

She smiled. "I'll head back over to check up on Dad."

"Good enough," Austin said. "It would be good if you could just stay inside the truck, but I don't think you're parked quite close enough for that."

"No, but it should be fine down there," she murmured,

as she walked toward the vehicle. She stopped, took another look back at him.

Austin shook his head. "I know. I'll be fine. Now go."

She gave him a ghost of a smile and quickly joined her injured father.

AS SOON AS Rox was out of sight, Austin pulled both Charlie and Cowboy back a little bit. Cowboy whined several times, but Austin whispered, "It's okay, buddy. I know, not quite the way you want to see this happen. You want to go see Jake," he murmured, "but I need you here for a bit."

He looked over at Charlie, grazing off to the side, completely unconcerned. Animals could be stressed during certain events, causing a high adrenaline rush. However, as soon as it was over, as the danger passed, they calmed down and went back to normalcy. Something that people could learn a lot from by observing the animal world.

With the animals tucked back a little bit farther out of the way, Austin could still keep an eye on not only what was in front of him but the world off to the side. He waited, hoping that law enforcement would show up first, knowing it would still be at least ten to twenty minutes and quite possibly longer than that. It's not that he didn't have a whole lot of faith in the local law, it's just that he had a bit more faith in the criminal element.

He pulled out his phone and quickly sent off several texts to Badger, updating him on what was currently breaking. When his phone vibrated, Austin answered the call and wasn't surprised to hear Badger say, "Do you need anything?"

"Some backup would be nice," he whispered. "Jake took a bullet to the shoulder, and I'm waiting for law enforcement now. I've contacted the oversight team that was here yesterday, and they're on their way too."

"Good. Any idea what size cache is still there?"

"I haven't seen it. I just know that our gunman mentioned *caches*, plural. So I guess it would be at least the same size if not bigger than yesterday's, and more than one are still out here."

"So, what the hell are they up to?"

"I think it's pretty obvious. I suspect these are local runners, connected to the big-time runners. These guys have been using Jake's place as a holding facility for a while because it's a relatively undisturbed area of the ranch. I think these local runners have somebody on the inside or at least had somebody at one time, somebody keeping track of Jake's place."

"You're thinking it's the ranch hands?"

"No, I'm not thinking it's them. Although I don't know the two current ranch hands. They're not the same guys who were here when I was here years ago. Yet I guess maybe one could be, though I never saw much of him as he was out riding the range most of the time," he shared. "As for our gunmen, there are at least three of them, one of which I've got here."

"Do you think there are any bad feelings among anybody in the immediate family?"

"If you think about it, nobody is on good terms all the time, but, from what I've seen, everybody appears to be decent, other than Chris, but what the hell do I know?"

At that, Badger snorted. "You know a hell of a lot, so don't ever doubt yourself in that corner."

"Oh, I might, but when you trust somebody once and get burned, you don't trust anybody ever again. You know, that kind of a deal."

"Is that how you feel about your wife?"

"No, not at all," he said, ending the call.

It didn't take long before he heard something in the bushes behind him. Cowboy growled softly. Austin gently eased his hand along the dog's back.

Cowboy went silent and nuzzled a little closer to him. Austin smiled at that, how Cowboy had become a combination of a pet and a working dog. He knew Cowboy was supposed to protect, and, in this case, he was also dealing with whatever had happened to him while he had been held captive.

Austin still didn't quite understand why they had done that, but suspected the reason was something simple. Sad, like so many things in life. Motivations ran hot when it came to these things. Unsure of what he heard, Austin waited and watched carefully, and, sure enough, it wasn't long before a man slipped through the trees, heading toward a section of the woods that Austin had yet to go into.

It was pretty hard to follow silently with both the horse and the dog, but it would be a good idea to know exactly what this guy was up to. Pulling out his phone, Austin videoed the man walking through the trees. The stranger then headed over toward one section of ground, a good one hundred yards away. Austin got as close as he could without getting close enough to be caught, then watched and waited.

The stranger bent down and quickly unburied what appeared to be a piece of plywood. He lifted it like a lid and looked inside, where Austin assumed would be another cache of weapons. He quickly put the plywood back down and covered it back up again. Then he went over to another area and went through the same motions, presumably checking on another cache of weapons. Interesting, just checking to ensure the goods were all still there. The fact that he was even checking was also interesting because he must have been worried about losing more of their goods. No matter what the reason, anything that caused these gun-runners to be pissed off was a good thing.

Austin watched and waited as the stranger quickly checked on three other caches, videoing him as he went. It would be a lot easier to find the weapons when this guy was gone. Just when Austin thought he was well hidden, a man called out.

"Did you catch that asshole?" The one guy checking the caches looked up and around. "I didn't see him."

"He's been watching you the whole fucking time, you idiot."

The other man froze. "No way, I would have seen him."

Sure enough, a man stepped around a tree, and he pointed out exactly where Austin was hiding. "He's in there. Go get him."

"I'm not going in there to get him," said the man checking on the caches. "You're the one who saw him. You go get him."

The other man glared at him. "Stop being such a fucking baby. We've got to get these weapons and get out of here."

"Not this trip. We didn't bring anything to haul them in, remember? We just came to check on them, and, so far, everything is here."

"Which just means you've shown this asshole where everything is. Now we can't give him the chance to tell anybody."

At that, the other man's lips pinched together, and he shook his head. "I'm not up for murder, and you know that."

"I don't give a shit what you're up for, but, with that attitude, you're destined to do some jail time."

"No need for that," he argued. "Just pay him off, as you do everybody else."

"I don't think this asshole is the paying-off type. He's the one who's been poking around in our business since he got back. Remember when we saw him that one time?"

"How do you know it's him? Are you telling me you saw him clear enough to identify him, but you didn't even let me know or go after him?" he asked in astonishment, as he stared at his buddy.

"Hey, this isn't my deal. Remember?"

"It sure as hell is your deal. You're the one who'll go to jail if we get caught," he declared, pointing a finger at him. "Now, go roust him out of there."

Austin listened with half a smile as the men continued to argue with each other. They probably knew he had a weapon and yet weren't telling the other one, each trying to get the other guy to go in after Austin.

Finally, when the two guys were just close enough together, Austin stepped forward, his rifle lifted, and announced, "Neither one of you have to check shit because I'm right here, and the two of you are just full of shit."

"We're not full of anything," the second man yelled.

Austin nodded. Sure enough it was the two he had braced earlier. "Friends of Chris, *huh*? So, who the hell is the other guy?"

"I don't know what you're talking about," muttered the

one man with the stubby nose. "We ain't done nothing wrong."

"One, you're trespassing, and, two, you're checking on caches of guns and probably drugs—on private property too. God only knows what else you're involved in."

"We aren't involved in anything," argued the younger, skinny guy.

Todd, but Austin preferred Stubby—nodded his head. "Yeah, we aren't involved in anything."

"Right, that's why you were just calling for him to come over and shoot me, *huh*?"

"I didn't say that," he stated in feigned innocence.

"No, no, of course not, and maybe my hearing is completely gone too. Don't worry though. I got it all recorded. I can check it later."

When the younger skinny man walked toward him, Austin lifted the rifle in his direction and muttered, "No you don't."

"You're not really going to shoot me out here, are you?" he asked in astonishment. "What the hell ever happened to this world that you'd just up and shoot people?"

"Yeah? Whatever happened to this world that you hide guns on a stranger's property?"

"He ain't no stranger," Skinny said.

"I don't get that. I really don't. I'm sure you guys think I should, but I don't understand why you're using Jake's place."

"Because it works," Stubby replied in astonishment. "How can it not make sense to you? Nobody's here, only a few cows, and we're not bothering anybody. Just miles and miles of range out here. Why not out there?"

Austin added, "At least here you have somebody who

can keep an eye on it once in a while."

"I didn't say that," Skinny muttered.

Stubby glared at him. "There you go, opening your fucking mouth again."

"I didn't say nothing," Skinny snapped, looking at his buddy.

Austin snorted. "Doesn't matter. This area is so close to the highway, anybody could be keeping track of what's going on here, and the fact that you say somebody *is* keeping track of it makes me wonder if you know that somebody."

At that, the two men looked confused.

Austin sighed. "Right, I guess I didn't explain myself very well."

"No, you sure as hell didn't," Stubby agreed, then laughed. "Look. Why don't you just head back to wherever the hell you came from and leave us alone."

"Really? What about the shooting that happened at the house today?"

The two men stared at each other, then turned to him. "You're from Jake's place?"

"Yeah, I am. What the hell did you think?"

Confused, they just looked at each other again.

"I told you at the pub that I was family. I'm Jake's son-in-law. Even if I wasn't from here, what difference does that make to you?"

"It just means you're ..." Then Stubby stopped again.

"One of the enemy?" Austin suggested.

"Kind of, yeah," he agreed, as he scratched the back of his head. "It does change things though."

"Why is that?" Austin asked.

"Because we didn't know you were here, for one."

"I don't think you care either," Austin noted. "You two

seem to be all about your gun stashes."

"I care. I'm not into killing," Skinny called out. "I know that's what my buddy here wants to happen, but I'm not really into that."

"That's nice," Austin noted, "but your buddy definitely is into that. So I'm not sure I believe you anyway, since you're here running guns."

"I'm just handing over the guns," Skinny clarified. "We're getting stuff in trade, and then we're selling that too."

"In other words, you're just moving goods."

"Exactly," Skinny confirmed, "and the guns aren't hurting anybody. They go into private collections, so whatever."

"Except that these aren't guns that you can buy at your local gun shop, even in Texas," Austin noted, with a laugh. "So why are you *not* bothered about weapons? Plus, drugs are in there too. Sounds like you are supplying drug cartels with the dope and the guns to protect their shipments."

"That's one of the other guy's sidelines," Skinny shared. "I don't handle drugs. That's bullshit. I don't handle the guns either. I just trade them."

"So, just what is it you're handling? What goods are you taking in as trade for the weapons?" Austin asked.

Skinny hesitated, looked back over at his buddy, Stubby.

Stubby shook his head at Skinny, warning him, "You better shut up. It'll get ugly if you don't."

Skinny dropped his gaze to the ground and muttered, "Yeah, I need to just stop talking."

"You think that'll make a difference?" Austin asked.

"It needs to because I didn't do anything wrong."

Austin shook his head. "I wonder, if push came to shove, and your buddy was charged with something, would he agree that you didn't do anything?"

At that, Stubby snorted. "He's every bit as involved as the rest of us. He just likes to think he's squeaky clean, but he's not. He just prefers a different line of products."

"Shut up," Skinny snapped, snarling at Stubby. "I'm not into drugs, and I'm not into selling guns, but they are a means to an end, and we've got other things we can sell."

"Yeah, and it's those *other things* you sell that I'm interested in," Austin stated, "because it's got to be something of value for you to go through all this."

He snorted. "Value that keeps on giving."

Now Stubby snorted at that. "You think you're so damn funny, but you open your mouth so damn much, and he'll figure it out."

Austin shook his head. "I already figured it out because the only thing that keeps on giving is women, and that will just piss me off if I find out you're into human trafficking."

"Not human trafficking," Skinny replied. "That sounds gross. We're just bringing aliens across the border, that's it. I get a few from the main shipment to parcel out here locally. Why do you even call them *aliens* anyway? That's what I don't understand. It's just women who are looking for work," he explained. "And so what if they don't get the work that they think they're getting? Most of the time they're so happy not to be reported that they don't even complain," he said, with a shrug.

"So, you're trading the weapons for women?" Austin asked, recording all the while.

"Yeah, for Mexican women, and sometimes other nationalities that whoever is running things on the border can grab."

"And nobody says anything?"

"Usually they don't have anybody. Besides, we treat them well. They get three meals a day, showers, beds to sleep in, and, hey, it's not as if it isn't the oldest profession in the world."

"That doesn't mean they're willing."

"Yeah, but they're not *unwilling*," he said, with a shrug. "Honest to God, most of them are happy just to have food."

Austin stared at them in disgust. "Really? Is that all it takes for *you* to be happy? Food? Clothes? Showers?"

"It makes them a lot happier," Skinny declared, looking at him. "Don't tell me that you've never been to a prostitute. Christ, this place is hot for it. We move the women all over, and it's pretty easy once we get them into the country, but we still have to have a source, and the source wants weapons, so that's what we trade with."

"*Right*." Austin would love to just beat the shit out of these two, but it wasn't to be.

"Besides," Skinny added, "not a whole lot you can do about it, and we're changing the operation anyway."

"Yeah? What change?"

"The women are also being moved," he shared. "It's getting a little too hot around this place. I don't understand why all of a sudden there's so much activity, but it's getting to be a pain in the ass. So we'll just move along closer to the border a bit. It's not as if there's too much of a problem doing that anyway. Unless they put up that whole wall, in which case we'll just find another way."

"That's the trick, isn't it?" Austin muttered, with a nod.

Skinny looked over at him. "Now just piss off so we can finish up what we've got to do here. Then we'll be gone, and you won't even see us again."

"So you say," Austin replied, staring at him, "but I'm

not sure I can believe you."

"Of course you can."

When a rustling came off to the side, the two men pulled out handguns and fired. Nothing came forth, but Austin sure as hell hoped it wasn't either Cowboy or Charlie. "You better not have shot my dog," he yelled.

At that, the two men looked at him. "Your dog?"

"Yeah, you know the one you kidnapped and kept penned up?"

"Jesus, he's a mean son of a bitch," Skinny muttered. "You've got to be crazy to have that dog."

"You were abusing it, locking it up when it didn't want to be locked up. Animals tend to not like people who treat them badly."

"Yeah, I know," Skinny agreed, giving him a toothless smile. "That's why I like the women who aren't particular."

"I thought you said you weren't abusing them."

"They're just women, another commodity, so give me a break," Skinny said, with a laugh. "I get it. You're probably one of those bleeding hearts who thinks everybody needs a fair chance, but I tell you these women are willing."

"Why is that?"

"Most of the time because they had some pressure on the other end to keep their family safe. That doesn't mean that anybody is threatening the family, but just the hint of that is usually enough to keep them in line." Skinny laughed. "Besides, it's none of your fucking business anyway."

It was like spinning on a dime, as his attitude changed completely, making it seem as if he was a good decade older than he had seemed earlier. In a better light Austin guessed Skinny could be late twenties to mid-thirties, but his friend Stubby over there had to be in his late forties already.

"I told you this guy is not somebody we want to leave hanging around," Stubby repeated.

"I heard you the first time," Skinny said. "The question is, what will we do with him?" He turned and looked back at his buddy. "You could have taken care of it already."

"Sure, I could, but I don't see you taking care of shit."

"Right, so you want me to get in trouble so you don't have to."

"Sounds good to me," Stubby replied, with a snort.

"You think any of us want more trouble?" Skinny asked his buddy.

"What kind of trouble have you had?" Austin asked Skinny.

"The big boss who does the major smuggling doesn't live around here, but he does little smuggling deals with our boss, the one we report to. So he acts as a middleman. Most of the time he's okay, but sometimes he's a piece of shit because he's got his own agenda. When people got their own agendas, that's when things go off the rail. He's got some revenge thing going on, and I ain't got much truck for that myself. If you've got a problem, get somebody to deal with it fair and square and upfront," Skinny suggested. "The rest of the time? Just put up and shut up." He laughed. "But then again, I'm the one making the big money here."

"We both are," Stubby declared, with a fat grin, but the grin fell off his face as he looked over at Austin. "Not that it matters to you."

"No, I get it. You running children too?"

"Only for adoptions," Skinny said, "and they're still not that easy to clear. The damn paperwork is a pain in the ass."

"Right, so more human trafficking," Austin muttered.

"I don't understand why that's a problem for you. People need a housekeeper, so they get a housekeeper. People want somebody to warm their bed, so they get somebody to warm their bed. If they've got money, they can get whatever they want. You should know that."

Unfortunately Austin found that to be a sad fact of life, and that was exactly what it was. Even as he was trying to figure out what to say next to keep these guys talking, he heard voices in the distance.

"Who the hell is that?" The men stared at each other and then immediately turned their handguns on him.

Austin shrugged. "You can both shoot me, but I'll still drop one of you first," he pointed out. "I'll make damn sure that you don't get back up again. So, which one will it be?"

The two men looked at each other, and Stubby frowned. "Oh, no fucking way you're doing that to me, buddy," he snapped. "I know all about your plans for getting out of this town."

"I do want to leave this town. It's not as if I've been hiding it," Skinny snapped right back. "I want to head west. Lots of opportunities for a guy like me out west."

"Sure, but it's pretty close-knit," Austin added. "They've got families out there who have been doing this for decades."

"Sure, but I bet I can find a pretty young thing to come over to my side, to join her knowledge with mine—and other things."

"You really think so?" Austin asked, with a smirk. "I don't."

"Why? What the fuck's wrong with me?"

"For one thing, your attitude toward women. They can smell that a mile away, unless you're planning on kidnapping and coercing them, and that won't go down too well with some papa bear."

"Whatever. … I don't care. I'll find something. Women are great to have as friends and all."

Austin smirked. "Until, when push comes to shove, you can't trust them."

"I'm not at all worried about that," Skinny bellowed. "This whole BS of revenge has me wondering about staying here any longer."

"Any idea why that middleman of yours has got revenge on his mind?"

"Yeah, something to do with his wife."

"His wife?" Austin repeated.

"Yeah, his wife. I think he's pretty stuck on the fact that she left him. Left him for somebody else, and took his son with her too."

"Well shit," Austin muttered, as an answer to this puzzle piece that he hadn't even considered as an option reared its ugly head. He knew it was more than time to put an end to this. "So, what'll it be, guys? That's law enforcement coming your way, pretty damn fast," he noted, as the noise picked up.

"What the hell?" Stubby grumbled, as he looked over at his buddy. "We have to get out of here. We also need the goods though," he added. "You know what'll happen to us if we lose them," he told Skinny.

"I wouldn't worry about that middleman boss you're talking about," Austin interjected in a conversational tone. "We'll pick him up in no time."

The men looked at him, then at each other, and Skinny shouted, "Fuck it, I'm not losing everything." He turned the gun in Austin's direction, but a sudden snap and a howl came from Skinny, as Cowboy leaped forward from the underbrush where he'd been sitting and took Skinny's gunhand down to the ground, pulling the man with it. Skinny continued to scream and to shout.

Meanwhile, Stubby froze for a second and then turned his gun on Austin too, but he was facing a shotgun.

"Go ahead and fire, asshole," Austin taunted him. "I'll make sure you're dead before you take another breath. Besides, your buddy here is going to hand over all the information that we could possibly want because I won't give him any medical treatment until we get that."

Stubby, his gaze narrowing cruelly, turned his gun and fired, shooting his buddy.

"Well fuck," Austin muttered, as he stared at Stubby. "That's a pretty low thing to do."

"He won't stop screaming, and, besides, he's been pissing me off, talking about how he'll make it in the big-time as soon as he gets out of here. He would never make it big-time. That guy's nothing but a piece of shit. Most of the girls he picks up he has to beat into compliance because, believe me, they aren't willing. I think it's a shit game."

"What's your game?"

"Nothing," Stubby spat. "I just make money on every deal I broker," he explained. "It's all about that for me, and then I'll get out of here."

"Really? How do you figure you'll do that?"

The guy lowered his handgun ever-so-slightly. "Because you're my ticket out of here," he shared, "and all I need is to get loose of this. I don't give a shit about the goods that you pick up here or the ones that are still hidden. I really don't give a crap. I'll hand over all the information, but I'm not sticking around to take the fall."

"You didn't have anything to do with the shooting at the house?"

"No, that was the piece of shit ... middleman, and you're right. It's all about revenge, ... but I don't know who all the players are. You better watch out though. That one's got a poisoned history."

"Yeah, I can see that," Austin said, "but that won't get you off the hook."

"It will if I pass everything I know over to you."

"You've got to make that deal with the feds, not me."

His eyes widened. "Feds, *huh*? That's not exactly the way I thought this would go."

"No, I'm sure it isn't, but, if you think you're getting out of here scot free, think again."

At that, Cowboy sat glaring at the body of his victim, but then his gaze now glommed onto the second man.

"I'll just shoot him, you know? If that dog comes after me, he's dead."

"Because you're the kind of guy who shoots animals."

"I kept it penned up, thinking he would be a good guard dog, then something about his ownership seemed to tick off our boss. He wanted the dog kept permanently because somebody else was suffering."

"Yeah, she was suffering all right. It was her dog."

"People are stupid to get hung up on emotional stuff. Then it just backfires on them."

"But not you, *huh*?"

"No, not me," he spat, his gaze narrowing as he watched him. "You can bet I'm not so fucked up that I care about that shit."

"No, you just care about yourself."

"Yeah, nobody else to care about. You need to remember that the world's messed up, and, just when you think you've got it straightened out, it gets even more messed up."

"You're not getting out of this."

"I won't talk to the feds. That's not happening."

"You've got a pretty long record, I'll bet."

"Don't matter what I got," he stated. "Some things we do in childhood just hang on to us."

"Some things that you do because you're an asshole hang on to you too."

Stubby gave him a sly smile and nodded. "You could be right, but they don't make deals with me, not when they figure out my history. So, absolutely no incentive to keeping you alive, and, if that damn dog comes my way, I'll enjoy taking care of him."

"You might," Austin conceded, "but I've still got my weapon, and, if you think I'll let you shoot my dog, you're wrong."

Stubby's eyes opened wide. "Another fucking animal lover? What the fuck is wrong with you?"

Stubby's movement had been so subtle, but Austin had seen it before. He knew what happened next, listening for it, and soon Stubby was sent flat to the ground, screaming in pain.

And, with that, two men in suits stepped out from the shrubbery, where they'd been waiting and watching. "That should have been a clean shot," muttered one of the suited guys.

"You could have stepped in and taken him down at any time, you know?" Austin noted.

But the fed frowned at him and asked, "Why? You had it handled. Besides, we were getting it on tape, so it's all good." He stepped closer to Stubby. "Too bad this one'll live. … I didn't account for the wind at the last minute. God knows it's all for best to just knock them on their ass permanently, and then we don't have to go through the court cases."

"Yeah," his partner agreed, "but Uncle Sam really likes it if we do it this way, as it gives him good numbers to spout out to the public that we're doing our jobs."

"Do your damn job then," Austin grumbled, as he glared down at the body on the ground, "because I'm done with this bullshit. There are also at least six caches of weapons here, so take them all."

"That is huge," Fed Number One agreed, with a big grin, "and it's all on video. We'll have to do a full search regardless."

Fed Number Two added, "Plus, we need to set up a sting to get the boss middleman and whoever else may be involved in running the women, the drugs, the guns."

Fed Number One pointed around. "We've got part of that handled. I'm not sure who this other boss is, but you can bet we need to find him too."

Austin nodded. "Yeah, you need to find him. I'm just not sure where," he added, "but I have a pretty damn good idea who it is."

Fed Number One turned to him and asked, "Who?"

"I think you'll find that it's Amie's ex-husband, Chris's biological father. And he'll be pissed even after all these years that Jake isn't handing off this whole ranch to Chris, or at least a controlling interest, because I think Chris's biological father figured it would put Chris and him on easy street. I'm pretty damn sure he's been planting that seed in his son's mind for a long time, and then all kinds of shit started to happen at Jake's place, revealing that things wouldn't go the way Chris thought they would."

"Which is just bullshit," Fed Number One replied. "Jake will never let anybody but family have this ranch."

"Sure, but, then again, I don't think Jake was expected to live very long."

Both feds nodded, as Fed Number One replied, "Right, and that makes sense."

Just then came a shout, and Austin turned to see several other team members joining them.

"Now," the federal agent noted, "you can take your animals and head back to the ranch, where you'll find a very pissed-off Jake, not to mention your wife—who is basically impossible to keep in line because she figures you are in some sort of trouble."

"Yeah, that's what being married is all about."

"Is it? I thought you guys were separated?"

"No," he corrected, "we just had to work out a few things."

"If that's what you call it," he muttered, "whatever."

Austin called to Charlie, who immediately stepped up. Austin hugged his favorite horse, then looked down at Cowboy and gave him a good scrub behind his ears. "I'll see you back at the ranch then."

"What about the other caches?" asked Fed Number One.

"I'm sending you my video right now. Go through it and you should see each spot from where you're standing right now. The sooner you get that shit out of here, the better. You might want to leave messages somewhere, like a big sign that reads *Hey, we found all of them,* which hopefully should get these assholes out of here permanently."

At that, the feds just laughed and nodded. "Sure, we can do something."

Austin added, "Let me know when you guys are through here. I'll have to come in behind you and fill up all the holes, so the animals don't fall into them."

The feds gave him a wave and brought up Austin's video on their phones.

At that, Austin hopped up on Charlie and called Cowboy to come back with him, and together they trotted for home.

CHAPTER 13

ROX WAITED ANXIOUSLY at the door. The feds had been all over the place all morning and had taken Austin in to the local station to get statements and to identify some stuff that apparently he'd seen—something about the video he had taken. He had to get things notarized or some bullshit. She didn't know what was going on, but she'd been pacing impatiently ever since.

Her father looked at her and muttered, "He'll be fine."

"Of course he'll be fine," she spat, with an eye roll. "It still doesn't change the fact that I don't like that they took him in with them."

"Sure, but he's a good man," Jake noted. When she glared at him, Jake added, "Hey, I'm just saying he's a good man."

"I know he is," Rox replied, easing back.

"Have you checked on your mother recently?" Jake asked.

Rox nodded. "She's still sleeping, which is good because it'll help stave off that migraine. Your getting shot didn't help her any either."

Jake just shrugged.

"How about Mom and you? How will that go?"

"It'll be fine," he said, "and it's just one of those things about life and marriage. ... I'm happy for you," he added suddenly.

She looked at him and smiled. "It's not a done deal yet," she murmured.

"Yes, it is," he declared, with a nod. "Austin knows what's good for him."

She stopped, turned, and frowned at her dad. "What do you mean? I know what's good for me too."

"Good for both of you," he agreed, with a smile, "but he's no fool, and he knows a good deal. As I told you, you've always been a great daughter, and I haven't been very good at letting you know it because I was so hooked on having a son for the longest time. But somehow, over these past five years, I completely forgot about that because I realized I didn't need a son because I already had you."

She stared at him in amazement as he went on.

"I know I'm not the smartest, and I'm sure as hell not the fastest at figuring shit out," he added, "but I do realize that I damaged something between us. Between me and Chris too. I didn't mean to do that, and I have to ask if you'll forgive me."

Tears immediately came to her eyes, and she wiped them away impatiently. "Of course, but you don't have anything to be forgiven for. You're allowed to want a son."

"Sure, I'm allowed to want a son," he conceded, "but not to the detriment of the family I already had and who loved me so much," he murmured. "I hurt you. I hurt Chris. I hurt your mother. That is one of the reasons why your mother and I had some problems. It was … I was a little too focused on what I thought I wanted, needed, liked, yet couldn't have," he admitted, "not being grateful for what I did have, and, for that, I'm sorry."

Rox walked over, bent down, and gave him a gentle hug.

His shoulder had been treated. As it turned out, the bullet creased his arm, resulting in a bad burn and several stitches, but wasn't nearly as bad as it could have been.

"I'm just sorry I was so thick-headed and stubborn, and I didn't get there before all this happened," Jake shared, "and, yes, I would have loved to have had a son with your mother, but, in reality, I have everything I could ever need."

Rox nodded, tears in her eyes. "Thank you, Dad," she whispered. "All I ever wanted was to be everything you needed, and being your son was the one thing I couldn't be."

"And you shouldn't have to," he said, with a headshake. "However, if you decided you want to keep that damn son-in-law of mine around, you won't get any complaints from me—but only if it's right for you."

She gave him a wry look. "That's another thing I'll need to work on with Austin. He's absolutely right for me, and I've grown and changed, and I am hopeful we can make a go of our marriage now," she shared. "It's been interesting having him here, and I couldn't have imagined the way this all came about."

"Me either," he muttered. "But you still need to do what's right for you, not craving the dream of the relationship from before because, if it ends up being something other than that dream, you won't be happy." Shaking his head, he added, "If all that didn't make sense, then let me say this. All I really want is for you to be happy."

He was saying absolutely everything she ever possibly wanted him to say, and he was doing it with such honesty that she knew it was coming from his heart. She gave him another gentle hug and said, "I'll keep it in mind, but I know that I never stopped loving Austin. In my heart I always expected him to come home."

"He did come home."

"But you know, he's kind of like some other people I know," she quipped, casting him a sideways glance as she stepped back. "They're a little stubborn at figuring things out too."

He gave her a grin. "Isn't that the truth?" Then he winced in pain as he shifted in the chair.

"Damn it, Dad, you'll have to baby that shoulder for a while," she muttered. "You don't get to cause all this chaos and then not look after it." He rolled his eyes. "Plus," she reminded him, "we're not out of danger until we can figure out what the hell is going on here."

"And that'll be the hard part," he said, "because, until that asshole sings, and we know for sure that he's the one behind all this, it's not over."

"I know," she agreed, "and that's what I mean. We've got to see it through."

"And we don't know what this will end up looking like, and it might not be pretty."

"It won't be pretty, I'm afraid," she said, "and just because Austin seems to think he knows who it is doesn't mean he's right."

"Everything has been so discombobulated, it's hard to know what's going on, but I hear what you're saying."

She poured him another cup of coffee. "Now Austin damn well better get his ass home again or …"

He laughed. "Or what? I remember when you used to say that after he left, and it took him five damn years to come home."

She nodded. "I said a lot of things back then, but now we've promised that I won't be issuing ultimatums and that, if I ever break that promise, he won't listen to me," she explained, with half a laugh.

"Sounds to me as if you've got some basics already ironed out."

"We do. We really do. It's been so nice to see him again, and it makes my heart feel good to know he's here, especially now."

"Yeah, and he's doing a lot for us. And if you guys can work out your stuff, then maybe your mom and I can work out ours too."

"Yeah," she muttered, "there's no excuses for anybody in this world."

He chuckled. "Even Chris, though he might be a different case. I'm not sure how much he's involved in all this, but he's still got a big damn chip on his shoulder."

"He sure does," she said, with a groan.

When the back door suddenly flung open, and somebody stepped inside, Rox frowned at the stranger and asked, "Can I help you?"

Her father slowly stood up. "Well, there you are. The dirty rat right from the beginning."

"What the hell?" Rox muttered, looking at the stranger and then finally understanding. "Joe?" she asked, with a frown, "You can't be Joe."

He looked at her and asked, "Why can't I be?"

He looked so different. "I didn't recognize you."

He shrugged. "That's normal for you guys, isn't it? Too high and mighty and too perfect to recognize the people below you."

She realized this was the man they suspected of being behind the gun caches being stored on their property. "Sounds like you and Chris have personal problems in the way you see things. ... So, you're the one behind all those guns being stored on Dad's property, *huh*?"

Joe shrugged. "Kind of, but not really. Business associates of mine were just looking for a location, and I was trying to make a bit of money, and they knew I was from around this area and had a connection to the ranch, so I could keep an eye on their supplies for them."

"Connection to the ranch?" Jake repeated, his voice dangerously low.

"Yeah, with my boy all set to inherit and all."

Jake asked, "What do you mean, Chris is all set to inherit?"

"That's how the will was supposed to be anyway. I wasn't going to kill everybody, but now that you went and had all the legals changed, I don't really have a whole lot of choice."

"What?" she asked. She turned to her father. "That's what the lawyer stuff was all about?"

"Yeah," he said, with a nod. "Did you kill my lawyer too?"

"No, but he was having a heart attack when I saw him. I just … didn't help and watched him die. It's a fascinating process really, and it gave me the chance to get all the paperwork we needed, transfer everything over to the new lawyer, and make a few changes. That is until you went and raided everything and screwed that all up. He's pissed at me over that."

"You think? Or did you decide you needed to get rid of him too?"

"I didn't get rid of anybody. He's on his way out of Texas anyway because he didn't want to get caught up in having done something illegal, which he certainly has done. It's not my problem. I didn't do it."

"You watched a man die and didn't render aid? That is a criminal offense," Rox pointed out, staring at him in disgust. "How could you do that?"

"It's not my fault, dear, and the guy was old, like, … really old."

"And you aren't?" she snapped.

He stiffened slightly. "You're pretty damn mouthy, aren't you? No wonder your brother hates your guts."

"Chris doesn't hate my guts," she declared, "and, if he does, it's because of the poison you've put in his head."

"I didn't have to put any poison in his head." Joe smiled and added, "Yet it's been fun to stoke the fire. He's been thinking this was his all this time. That this whole ranch was his."

"Because you told him so, I suppose."

"It should have been his. There's nothing wrong with my boy, and he should have it, but just because you wanted your own spawn in here, that doesn't mean Chris should have been kicked out."

"He wasn't kicked out," Jake corrected him. "I cut him in for quite a large share."

"But not a controlling interest, so he won't get anything but his share of the work," Joe pointed out, "and that's not what he was in for. I wanted my boy to have the biggest and the best ranch around."

"Yeah, and why is that?" Rox asked.

"Why not? After all … this asshole took your mother away from me. They had an affair while we were still married. Did you know that? Then they went away on a holiday hunting trip, and she comes back all ready to leave me."

"And you beat her up pretty good for that too, didn't

you?" Jake asked, staring at him. "I still owe you for that."

"Whatever. I didn't really care about her leaving, but I didn't want her taking my boy and then turning him against me."

"Hardly," Jake countered. "She did everything she could to keep the family intact, to keep you seeing Chris, to keep you in his life."

"Yeah, and believe me that I returned the favor by letting him know exactly what marrying in this family meant. I told him I only allowed it to happen because you would give the farm to him and nobody else."

"What the hell?" Jake asked, staring at him. "Why would you do that?"

"Because I figured it would come to him. It is possible, ain't it?" And, with a sudden movement, a handgun slid out of his sleeve into his palm. "With you dead, that just leaves his mother and his sister, and they're completely incapable of doing anything. I figured you for the protective kind, which is why I was so surprised to find that my boy got cut out of the will."

"He didn't get cut out," Jake growled, between clenched teeth.

"Close enough, but, with you gone, it'll be his anyway. He's not behind my doing this. I am, so it's not as if he can be pinned for this, so, if his sister's gone as well, that's even better, isn't it?"

"Why is that?" Rox asked.

"Because then he gets 100 percent of the ranch," Joe stated in a mocking voice, "and he doesn't have to worry about being jealous of you for the rest of his life." The handgun was raised and wafted back and forth between the two of them. "Now which one should go first?"

"How about neither of us?" she snapped. "I can't believe Chris would even listen to you spouting all these lies."

"These so-called lies are about to become true. You can sure as hell bet that Chris won't mind when the dust falls, and he's left owning this entire place."

"Jesus Christ, you are fucking out of your mind," Rox declared, staring at him.

"Good Lord, listen to that mouth on you?" Joe stared at her. "That's just gross. Your mama has really slipped if that's how she's raising her daughter." And that just made Rox even madder. He nodded. "I can see the temper on you, … that's Jake all over again." Joe laughed. "You think I don't know what your father was like?"

Rox just glared at the man.

"He was hell on wheels when he was younger, but now he's old, just like everybody else, even me," Joe admitted. "We all get old, just not as old as that lawyer." He gave a mock shudder. "*Ugh*, that was just gross."

"Gross that he died?" she asked, studying Joe as if he were an insect, one she didn't understand.

"Sure, he got old, and he died, but he should have died earlier. It would have been easier on everybody."

"But he didn't, and apparently the way it went turned out to be very convenient for you."

"I will admit it was convenient," Joe said. "You got that right." He laughed and then added, "You know, the first bullet goes to Jake." He looked over at her and smiled. "That's because I know you'll be so much easier to deal with, with your daddy down. Plus, he's always been somebody you didn't want to brace in the dark."

"You still don't," she muttered, straightening up and stepping in front of her father. In the distance she heard sounds but wasn't sure what direction it came from. When a bark came outside, she realized it was Cowboy. She recognized her father stiffening at the sound too because Cowboy had gone into town with Austin, seemingly not wanting to be separated from him. She may have found her dog again, but no doubt, as far as Cowboy was concerned, he was more attached to Austin than anybody else.

She wasn't exactly sure what would happen when Austin got into the house, but it would get ugly and very quickly. She waited, tense and ready for whatever would happen, but when the back kitchen door slammed shut there was no sign of Austin. No sign of Cowboy.

Joe spun around, glanced back at them, and asked, "Who the hell is there?"

"No clue," Rox replied, trying to keep her facial expression innocent and bewildered, when suddenly the back door slammed again.

"I ain't playing fucking games," Joe yelled, as he stepped to the door and opened it. "Whoever is out there, get your ass inside, or I'll start shooting people."

Just then, Austin stepped in with Cowboy at his side. Cowboy looked up at the newcomer and growled.

"Ah, so you're the one who kept him penned up, aren't you?" Austin asked.

"I'm the one who kidnapped him and insisted the guys keep him penned up. I knew the damn dog was hers, and her brother wanted her to suffer, so I figured that was just another little twist we could add for Chris's revenge."

"And he was okay with that?" Rox asked Joe.

"I don't think he even knew about it. All that kid's been doing is moaning and groaning about being separated from his family and all his friends. Just bitching and whining because he's been wanting to come back and be friendly with the whole lot of you, but I've been trying to get his head straight through this whole thing, telling him that's not the way to go about getting the ranch."

"Maybe he doesn't even want it," she pointed out. "Did you ever think about that?"

"Doesn't matter if he wants it or not. My boy is getting it. He's my boy, and my boy is getting this place. Do you hear me? I didn't just lose your mother, you know? It was also this bloody inheritance."

"What are you talking about?" she asked, her gaze going from Joe to her dad.

"What he's talking about is the fact that his family owns one of the connecting ranches about ten miles over," Jake explained, "and they sold a big chunk to my father way back when."

"That's right, but it wasn't fair, and you know it." Joe glared at him.

"Your dad was having a hard time, and they made a deal that was fair," Jake snapped. "I'm tired of listening to your innuendoes about how we stole it from you."

"You fucking did," Joe yelled, "and I'm fucking tired of listening to you lie about it."

Jake groaned. "Just more of the same old thing. Joe, all you do is complain, and you wonder why Chris is like that? I've told you over and over, Joe. My family didn't steal any land from you, and I didn't steal your wife either."

"You sure did," Joe bellowed. "She never would have left me without you in the picture."

"She left you because you were an asshole and beat her. She chose me over your sorry ass. I don't beat my wife. I treat her well."

"She wasn't a very good wife," Joe replied, with a shrug. "So, what if she needed a little tuning up?"

At that, Rox felt her own anger burning. She took two steps forward, glaring at Joe. "You beat up my mom?"

"What the hell?" he asked, looking at her. "Don't you look all high and mighty, as if you're something special. You're not, so just deal with it."

"Thanks for that," she said, with a laugh. "I never really worried about being special. I just wanted to be enough."

"That's all anybody ever wants," Joe noted in a mocking tone, "and what nobody ever is, so just knock it off." He motioned at Cowboy. "At least the dog knows me."

Austin nodded. "He certainly knows of you. He's not sure who and what you are yet, and that's something he'll have to work out on his own," Austin stated, as he eyed Joe's gun. "Is that one of the guns from the stash?"

He glanced at it and shrugged. "A shit ton of weapons were right there, so why the hell wouldn't I take one? You can buy anything you want here, but it's still better if you don't have to pay for it." Then he laughed. "Besides, these aren't registered, so it's all the better." He looked over at Jake and raised the tilt of his handgun. "I've been waiting for this moment for a very long time."

"Because all you've ever wanted to do was get rid of me? So, you've spent half your life thinking about nothing but revenge?" Jake asked Joe.

"Yeah, revenge is one of the best things," Joe replied, "especially when you finally get around to getting it."

"That's what this is all about, isn't it?" Austin asked, staring at him. "It's not even about Chris, is it? This is all about you getting back at Jake."

"Whatever," Joe muttered. "It is about Chris. It's about

making sure that Chris gets exactly he wants."

"Chris doesn't want the ranch," said a man from the doorway. "What the hell are you doing, Dad? I told you that I wanted to be a part of it, but I really didn't. I don't want to run a ranch or even to work on one. I want to have my own mechanic's shop in town. I don't have the money to do that, and I wouldn't get cashed out anyway because there is no cash here. It's a working ranch, and they need everything they have to keep it going. You always hyped up everything and made it seem as if I would get a big huge chunk at the end of the day."

"Sure you will," Joe declared. "Stick by me, and you'll be fine, son. We'll get you this ranch, and you won't have to run the place. You can sell it. That was the whole plan. You get the whole place, and then you can sell it. Then we can watch every one of these losers rolling over in their graves in agony."

Chris stared at him. "No way we can sell this. It's been in Jake's family forever."

"But not *your* family, and, as long as you're the one who gets it at the end of the day, nothing else matters."

Chris looked over at Rox. "I didn't set this up," he said, raising his hand as if swearing on a Bible. "I just heard in town what the hell was going on. I knew about some of it, about the weapons being stashed, and I'll admit to knowing about that." He shook his head. "I still wasn't a part of it."

"I don't think anybody will believe you now," Rox said, frowning at him. "You're way too far into this nightmare."

"I'm not though. I haven't done anything."

"Yeah, well, standing by and not saying anything is doing plenty," she declared, glaring at him. "You know they shot Dad, right?"

He looked over at his stepfather and winced. "Jesus. No, I didn't know that." He took a hesitant step forward as he looked at Jake. "I'm sorry. I should have told you before it came to this."

Jake just glared at him, then reluctantly nodded. "I didn't think you would be a part of it, but I wasn't sure, not when we saw how bad things were getting."

"It wasn't anything to do with me, I swear to God. It wasn't," he said almost desperately.

"Shut up," Joe roared. "I told you before how I don't like all that whining."

"I know you don't," Chris snapped. "You don't like anything about me. All I've ever been to you was a tool, a way to get back at Jake, and I didn't even see it in time to do anything about it. You've just been using me, and you've lied to me, turning me against them. They've been nothing but good to me, and all I've been to them is a jerk. A lousy stepson, a lousy son to poor Mom, and a lousy brother to Rox," Chris admitted. "I've been so angry I couldn't see what was really happening."

"And what? Now you've suddenly seen the light?" Joe asked mockingly.

"Yeah, I've kept myself drunk and loaded so I wouldn't have to deal with it, but I'm sober now, and I can see for myself what the hell has really been going on right under my nose," he declared defiantly. "Do you know what some of those guys have been doing? The guns aren't the half of it."

"Quit your sniveling bullshit," Joe bellowed. "As I told you before, we'll get the ranch for you, we'll sell it, and everything will be fine."

"I don't want to sell it. It belongs to this family, and Rox is the one who should end up running it. It's her place and always has been. She's worked hard her whole life on this ranch, and it's very much where she wants to be and what she wants to do."

"That's just too fucking bad," Joe snapped, "because I won't let my place stay in her hands."

He raised his handgun toward Jake, but Chris stepped right in front of him. "No, Dad. That's enough of this bullshit. You're letting your own anger and hatred cause all this."

"I don't give a fuck what you think. Now move your ass before I shoot you too."

Squaring his shoulders, Chris leaned forward and glared at his father. "Then shoot me," he dared Joe. "Why the hell not? Everything else in my world is pretty well fucked up now anyway."

Joe glared at him and pushed the gun directly into his belly.

Immediately Austin yelled, "This has gone way too far." He looked over at Chris and nodded. "Thanks for coming, Chris."

"I wasn't ready to hear what you had to say at first, but I eventually got your message," he said. "Almost too late, it seems. However, once you showed up, everything changed. It was just like old times, and, like always, it pissed me off. Yet you could always talk to me, Austin, even when I couldn't talk to myself, and that's bullshit too," he muttered, as he shook his head, his gaze going back to his father. "Dad, this has gone on for far too long, and it needs to stop."

"Oh, it'll stop all right. It'll end here today." Joe took a step back, raised the gun until it was pointed right under his son's jawline and growled, "Now you fucking move."

Austin stepped forward, beside Chris, and said, "Leave Chris alone."

The gun switched to him, as Austin just smiled—and in a move that Rox had never seen before—he did something with his foot that pulled Joe forward, right into Austin's fist. The gun didn't even go off, but it went down with Joe, and Austin's boot followed onto Joe's gun hand, crunching bones. Joe screamed, as Austin bent down and removed the handgun from his fingers and handed it off to Jake. "That's part of the cache, so be sure the feds get it," he stated, with a warning look at Jake.

Jake glared at him, then down at the man who'd brought this all to his family.

Austin shook his head. "No, Jake, it stops now."

Jake glared hard for a few seconds, but Amie stepped into the room, her voice soft as she said, "Leave it be, Jake."

He looked over at her, and his shoulders sagged as he nodded. He quickly removed the bullets from the gun, put everything on the table, and pulled out his phone. "This fucking better be over now," he muttered. "I'm damn tired of this shit."

Then he walked into the other room to make the call.

MUCH LATER THAT evening, everybody had a chance to air their views. It ended so late that Chris was even spending the night, while they all tried to process the events of the day. As Austin hopped out of a shower, not very quickly and definitely not easily, he put his prosthetic partway on his leg, grabbed a towel and wrapped it around his waist, as he hobbled out of the bathroom and over to his room. As he got to his door, the door beside him opened, and there was Rox in a nightie.

"Come on in here," she said. When he hesitated, she shook her head. "No way. I'm not sleeping alone tonight."

"I thought we were going to take it slow."

"You can take it slow," she replied, with a nod, "but I have no intention of it."

He headed her way, saying, "Look. … I'm … It's not pretty."

"I don't give a shit about pretty," she stated. "I've seen so much more of you these last few days. More than I ever saw before. I don't care about whatever it is you are worried about. I just know that I don't ever want to see you facing down a gun again."

"That's a good thing," he quipped, "because it's really not on my to-do list either."

She looked at him briefly and cracked a smile. "That was another one of the things you were always really good at."

"What?"

"Deflecting a tough situation with humor."

"Sometimes it makes things easier." He managed to get into her room and collapsed onto the side of the bed.

She looked at his leg and asked, "Do you need to take that off?"

"Yeah, for sleeping I do. Plus, it's good to have it off for a while."

"Then take it off now," she replied.

It came off quickly since he hadn't put it on properly in the first place. Lowering it to the floor, he rubbed his stump.

She stepped forward and critically examined his leg. "It looks puffy and sore. What do we need to do for that?"

"Some cream helps, but I didn't bring it. It wasn't exactly normal duty today," he noted, with half a smile.

"So, Kat is the one who built that for you?"

He nodded. "Yeah, we're constantly working on new designs. I figure, by the time she's finished working her magic on this one, I should be in really good shape. She's always working on new and better designs."

"I suspect this is the kind of thing that you're never set for good on, are you?"

"I don't know," he murmured. "I prefer to think that I'll get it to the point where everything is good enough."

"No, not you," she argued. "You'll still be striving to get a better leg, better movement, or better whatever it is you think you need."

"It's not even so much about *need*," he pointed out. "I just want to be back to as good as I was before."

"You have metal sticking out of your leg," she noted, frowning at him.

He nodded. "I had osseointegration surgery where that titanium was implanted. They make it for the prosthetic, so it's a whole lot easier to get it on and off."

She nodded slowly. "Wow, there's a whole world here I hadn't even considered."

"If you're serious about wanting to try again with me," Austin began, "this is how I come."

"Good. I wouldn't have it any other way." She gave him a gentle push backward, so that he was stretched out on her bed.

"Are you sure?" he asked, as she scooched down beside him. He watched the smile in her eyes grow and deepen, as he sighed happily. "You know we don't have to."

"I know that, but I figured that, with everything else going on tonight, nobody would care either way. However, I care. I care so much, and I knew that we came awfully close to losing each other today," she added. "I don't want to go through that again."

He nodded and pulled her close and gave her a gentle kiss.

"Besides," she muttered, "I also had no clue about your leg, and I wanted to know if you would be comfortable enough to share it with me."

"I wasn't planning on spending the rest of my life hiding in the bathroom. You can bet on that."

She grinned. "No, I can't imagine that either, although it might be fun to try."

"Nope," he said, shaking his head. "No more hiding, no more lack of communication, everything open and above-board. This is the leg. This is how it is. If you can't deal with it, you need to tell me now. If you look closely, you'll find plenty of new scars since you saw me last, so you might as well check all that out too."

She shook her head. "Stop it. You're fine. You are gorgeous just the way you are." He burst out laughing, and she grinned. "See? You always used to laugh when I said things like that, but I mean it. You're one of the really beautiful people in the world, both inside and out." She placed a finger against his lips when he went to crack a joke. "No, I mean it."

He nodded. "Thank you. I'm not used to hearing compliments."

"I know," she said, "and it's one of the saddest things in our lives. We're really good at knocking each other, but we're not very good at building each other up or at reminding each other when we've done something great, but these last few days have been great." She leaned over, lightly kissed him, and then deepened it.

Just like he remembered.

When he groaned, she lifted her head and asked, "Did I hurt you?"

He laughed. "Isn't that my line?"

"Nope. I know you're not injured," she replied, putting air quotes around that last word, "but I don't want to hurt you either."

"Honey, I don't hurt that easily," he replied, "so you're doing just fine."

"Good," she said, as she waggled her eyebrows. "I just wanted to know that we're still good to play."

"We're still good to play," he agreed, with a big grin, as he pulled her on top and shifted so they were lying more side by side. "I might be missing part of my leg, but everything else works just fine."

She laughed. "I wasn't going to say anything, but I figured you weren't stopping me, so everything must be functioning."

"I wouldn't be here otherwise."

She stopped and glared at him. "Even if everything wasn't functioning, that isn't the end of the world," she declared, "although I'm grateful that everything is intact because I do want kids."

"I know, and so do I … someday," he added, with a warning note.

"Someday could be sooner than you think," she teased, "because I don't have any protection."

"That's all right," he said. "We'll take life it as it comes."

And, with that, he rolled over, stretched out on top of her, his weight on his elbows, as he looked down at her and whispered, "I am so damn glad I came to find Cowboy."

"And I'm so damn glad too," she muttered, "that I put out the message to the War Department that he was missing."

He nodded. "Now if only I had some way of knowing if Kat really understood what she started."

Rox replied, a twinkle in her eye, "Oh, I think she does."

"Why is that?"

"Because I contacted her."

He stared at her in shock.

Rox shrugged. "The War Department told me that she was involved in handling issues with War Dogs, so I contacted her, told her where I was and what was happening. She mentioned that she might know somebody who could come who happened to be familiar with this area. I asked if by chance it happened to be a guy named Austin, and, if so, that she should tell him to get home where he belonged."

He stared at her, lifting up even higher to study her expression.

She nodded. "I'm not kidding. I'm sure Kat will back me up."

He just stared at her and started to chuckle. Soon, he was laughing so hard that he rolled off onto the bed beside her. "Oh my God, if that doesn't beat all."

"I'm serious," Rox stated. "It was definitely time for you to come home. I just couldn't figure out how to tell you."

"You could have just picked up the phone."

"I did," she teased, with a quirky smile in his direction. "Just maybe not calling you directly, but calling the person you would listen to. Plus, it made for a hell of a good reason to send you here."

"Convenient that Cowboy was kidnapped when he was."

"Don't you even dare think such a thing. You know I

would never hurt an animal. Personally, I get on better with animals than people."

He placed a finger on her lips. "Stop, all that is over now. Whatever that was, it's over, and now we're moving on to a whole new world."

She smiled. "Glad to hear it. Don't you think that we should maybe spend a little less time talking and a whole lot more time on something else?"

He smiled, opened his arms, and pulled her into his embrace. "Personally, I would have been okay if we hadn't talked at all."

He lowered his head and kissed her the way he'd been wanting to ever since he'd first set eyes on her again.

CHAPTER 14

ROX'S TOES CURLED, her breath came out in short cries and gasps, and, when Austin finally lifted his head, she whispered, "God, it's been so long."

"I know, Jesus."

She stopped, stared at him, and he nodded.

"Yes, because, as far as I was concerned, … I was still married. It's just that my wife was very stubborn."

She grinned. "Yeah, I think *very stubborn* is quite true." She pulled him down and gave him a searing kiss of her own, setting free all the pent-up emotions, frustration, and love that she'd been holding back for so long.

Before she realized it, they were both completely nude, stretched out on the bed, her arms over her head, as he carefully worked to awaken all her sensitive spots that had been dormant for so long, and now were springing to life with a vengeance.

"Good God," she whispered, twisting in his arms.

"I know," he whispered, "hold on."

"No, I'm not going to wait any longer."

"I'm here," he whispered, shifting in her arms, and then he was inside her, exactly where he belonged. He froze above her, and she froze beneath him. They looked at each other, and tears came to her eyes.

He lowered his head, kissed away the tears, and whispered, "Why the tears?"

"Because I waited so damn long for you to come home, and now you're here, … and it feels so damn right."

She cried out as he surged deeper into her and set a pace that was crushing, until she felt ripped apart in his arms, wondering at the safety of the port he offered amid the craziness of her world.

When he collapsed beside her, she whispered, "Please don't ever leave me again."

"Never," he murmured back, "not even if you send me away."

She looked over at him. "I'm so sorry."

"I know, and so am I. We were both at fault, and neither one of us was ready to make amends, and now? … We've both grown, and we're here together, ready to rebuild our lives."

She wrapped her arms around him and whispered, "Only if you're in it with me. I only want a future that has you right beside me."

"Done," he declared. "That is the perfect plan for both of us."

EPILOGUE

KAT STARED AT Badger, a big grin on her face. "It really worked," she crowed.

He just shook his head. "I can't believe it, and Rox actually called you?"

"I knew about Austin, and she knew about Austin, so you know about stubbornness. Sometimes you just have to try to get people to do something that maybe they didn't think they should do," she explained, followed by a laugh, "but I am thrilled."

"So am I." Badger shook his head. "Just amazing. So is there only one more?"

"Only one, at least for the moment," she clarified, as she looked at the file in front of them.

Badger asked, "You've got Mateo for this one?"

"I do, and I've asked him about it, but I haven't really told him what it is."

"Of course not, but you may want to give him a heads-up though."

"He told me that he's ready for anything. He just needs to get out and to find something else to do with his life. So, I thought this might be a good one for him."

"Maybe, maybe it is. Where is it?"

"In Virginia," she replied. "I don't even have very much. I just have the adopted family and a note saying that a wellness check didn't show any signs of anybody being there."

"So, we don't know what happened?"

"I followed up with the local police, and all they had was that the entire family has gone missing."

"The entire family?"

"Yeah." Kat nodded, looking at Badger worriedly. "As in, from one day to the next, nobody has seen them. The vehicle is still there but nothing else."

"Murdered?"

"We don't know, but …"

"What about anybody else? Anybody got anything?"

Kat sighed. "One of the neighbors mentioned a young woman had come and gone a couple times, trying to raise some attention to the case, but I'm not sure that anybody was necessarily looking into it to her satisfaction. So I'll put Mateo in touch with her, and we'll see if we can get this one solved too."

"I would hate to think the last one would beat us," Badger muttered.

"It won't," Kat declared.

Badger walked closer and wrapped his arms around her. "I have faith in you."

She smiled up at her husband. "That could be misplaced faith."

"It could be, but, even if so, it's still good."

"We have done something … really phenomenal."

He stopped, then laughed. "No, *you* have done something phenomenal. So, trust in that and rejoice. We'll see this one through and then see what happens. So far you haven't been wrong yet."

She grinned at him, a twinkle in her eye. "Let's hope I'm not this time either."

This concludes Book 29 of The K9 Files: Austin.

Read about Mateo: The K9 Files, Book 30

The K9 Files: Mateo (Book #30)

Welcome to the all new K9 Files series reconnecting readers with the unforgettable men from SEALs of Steel in a new series of action packed, page turning romantic suspense that fans have come to expect from USA TODAY Bestselling author Dale Mayer. Pssst... you'll meet other favorite characters from SEALs of Honor and Heroes for Hire too!

Mateo is always ready to help, especially when it comes to animals. When Kat, her War Dog files in hand, suggests he find out what happened to Thorny, the latest missing K9 dog, Mateo eagerly agrees. But it's not just the dog that's missing—the entire family has vanished, and the reasons are unexpectedly complex.

Maraya, with a heart full of concern, has been trying to get anyone to care about the missing family next door. Her tarnished reputation in town makes it difficult, and a welfare check leads nowhere when no one answers the door.

Thorny is eventually found in the woods, fiercely guarding a small boy from the missing family. This discovery

sparks interest—but not in a good way. As Mateo and
Maraya delve deeper, they uncover hidden secrets and a
budding romance, adding layers of intrigue to their quest.

Find Book 30 here!
To find out more visit Dale Mayer's website.
https://geni.us/DMSMateo

Author's Note

Thank you for reading Austin: The K9 Files, Book 29! If you enjoyed the book, please take a moment and leave a short review.

Dear reader,

I love to hear from readers, and you can contact me at my website: www.dalemayer.com or at my Facebook author page. To be informed of new releases and special offers, sign up for my newsletter or follow me on BookBub. And if you are interested in joining Dale Mayer's Reader Group, here is the Facebook sign up page.
http://geni.us/DaleMayerFBGroup

Cheers,
Dale Mayer

About the Author

Dale Mayer is a *USA Today* best-selling author, best known for her SEALs military romances, her Psychic Visions series, and her Lovely Lethal Garden cozy series. Her contemporary romances are raw and full of passion and emotion (Broken But … Mending, Hathaway House series). Her thrillers will keep you guessing (Kate Morgan, By Death series), and her romantic comedies will keep you giggling (*It's a Dog's Life*, a stand-alone novella; and the Broken Protocols series, starring Charming Marvin, the cat).

Dale honors the stories that come to her—and some of them are crazy, break all the rules and cross multiple genres!

To go with her fiction, she also writes nonfiction in many different fields, with books available on résumé writing, companion gardening, and the US mortgage system. All her books are available in print and ebook format.

Connect with Dale Mayer Online

Dale's Website – www.dalemayer.com
Twitter – @DaleMayer
Facebook Page – geni.us/DaleMayerFBFanPage
Facebook Group – geni.us/DaleMayerFBGroup
BookBub – geni.us/DaleMayerBookbub
Instagram – geni.us/DaleMayerInstagram
Goodreads – geni.us/DaleMayerGoodreads
Newsletter – geni.us/DaleNews

www.ingramcontent.com/pod-product-compliance
Lightning Source LLC
Chambersburg PA
CBHW070627170726
48291CB00003B/903